CAN'T HELP THE WAY THAT I FEEL

SULTRY STORIES OF AFRICAN AMERICAN LOVE, LUST AND FANTASY

EDITED BY
LORI BRYANT-WOOLRIDGE

CLEIS PRESS

Published in the United States by Cleis Press Inc., 2246 Sixth St., Berkeley, California 94710.

Printed in the United States.
Cover design: Scott Idleman
Cover photograph: Mark Scott/Getty Images
Text design: Frank Wiedemann
Cleis Press logo art: Juana Alicia
First Edition.
10 9 8 7 6 5 4 3 2 1

ISBN: 978-1-57344-386-9

Contents

INTRODUCTION: LEAD ME INTO TEMPTATION

We usually know what we can do, but temptation shows us who we are.

—Thomas à Kempis

A woman's desires are as multifaceted as her shoe collection. There are times when she craves romance and sensuality and wants her sex to reflect that. Then there are nights when she wishes to be the temptress—the bad girl—and take what she wants, when she wants it. Sometimes the real world just isn't enough and getting carried away by her fantasies can be the perfect aphrodisiac, allowing her to take matters into her own capable hands. And sometimes, temptation takes the form of something totally forbidden or unimaginable....

Can't Help the Way That I Feel is a collection of titillating stories, each written around a delicious enticement that stretches the boundaries of good-girl decorum and explores the idea that some temptations are just too tantalizing to ignore.

Ever since Eve seduced Adam into biting that apple, avoiding temptation has been drilled into our heads as the proper thing to do. But I ask you, can't giving in to temptation be a *good* thing sometimes (chocolate, shoes and Denzel immediately come to mind)? Must we *always* avoid enticement? If so, why?

Consider this: a little temptation can be a very good thing because sometimes it acts as a catalyst for our personal growth. Sometimes in an impulsive moment, we find ourselves growing into the next version of ourselves—our more open, spontaneous, courageous, adventurous, curious, fabulous selves.

I've come to believe that many temptations we encounter are actually whispers of restless discontent attempting to lure us into questioning the status quo areas of our lives. Quite often sex is such an area. Sex is the thing that we are the most curious and yet the least confident about. When it comes to sex our will to be good—to avoid temptation—often stands firmly in the way of our wants, needs and desires, without us ever really questioning *why* denial is the right thing to do.

In the stories that follow, you will meet several compelling characters who share some of your same feelings about their love and sex lives—boredom, confusion, dissatisfaction, prudence. And like yours, each of their journeys is different. But unlike most of us, they decide to take control of their hot sexy selves. Each woman finds herself giving in to temptation, and in its aftermath, learning something about herself, and growing into the woman she wants to be.

Take Livia ("What Would Quincy Do?"), a divorced, celibate, cancer survivor, who while hiding behind her supersexy alter ego, creates her own bucket list of temptations in order to climb out of survivor mode and bring joy, passion and pleasure into her life. Or Gracie ("Bubble Music"), a God-fearing Georgia peach, who hard as she tries, can't resist getting her hands dirty at an erotic art party, only to learn that God works in mysterious and often pleasurable ways. There's Sheila ("Tandem"), a woman in desperate need of a man's touch, whose birthday massage turns into a decidedly lusty temptation when a dynamic duo of masseurs rub her in all the right ways. Then there's Lissa ("Sangria Seduction"), who drinks from the forbidden cup of lemon sangria, which becomes the elixir of lust for one playah trying to seduce the naughty out of one very nice girl. And you'll meet Genevieve ("Translation Sensation"), an adventurous French tourist visiting New York, who learns that the language barrier can tempt a girl into some seriously sexy situations, and that lust is truly an international tongue.

These characters, and a host of others, will tickle your fancy and ignite your lust as you live vicariously through their enticing sexcapades. And after they have you and your imagination revved up and ready to purr, let us "Lead You Into Temptation" with three tasty, to-be-continued story starters designed to get your creative (and other) juices flowing and tempt you into making this erotic tome uniquely personal by finishing your own sexy tale on the blank pages provided. Don't feel the need to finish these stories on your own. Grab your favorite lover and spend the night researching and then writing your personal erotic tale together. You'll also have fun trying to figure out which of your favorite authors wrote these yummy bites for your creative pleasure.

And speaking of authors, I want to pay homage to the writers who contributed to this collection. My name is on the cover, but it is their creativity, imagination and courage that have made this anthology a high-quality work of erotic storytelling. I so appreciate their talent and professionalism and I encourage you to search them out and read their other work. You won't be disappointed.

I also want to thank my amazing agent, Sara Camilli. Every author should be so lucky. And thank you Brenda Knight and the fabulous art department at Cleis Press for the beautiful cover.

Now before I turn you loose to delve into the sultry tales that await you, I must offer this disclaimer: SAFE IS SEXY! The majority of these stories do not include condoms and other safe sex measures, but you know as well as I do that no temptation is worth risking your health for. So be smart. Be prepared. And always, always be safe.

Now turn the page and give in to the temptation to be yourself, to live your life (and sex life) on your own terms, by your own truth. Trust me, some temptations can be a very, very good thing.

Lori Bryant-Woolridge

WHAT WOULD QUINCY DO?

Elle

I think great erotica should be like Braille—a must-touch reading experience.

—Elle

Have you tried giving him a professional?" the radio diva boldly asked her caller.

"They always work for me," chimed in her streetwise male sidekick.

"A professional what?" I queried aloud. Though I had not expected a response, sucking sounds, intermingled with soft grunts supplied by the special effects button, were the reply. So this is what relationship advice had come down to in the new millennium? Was a blow job now the modern-day Band-Aid for whatever ailed him?

"The real question is: Has he tried giving *her* a professional? Why does it always have to be the woman doing the giving? Thank god I'm old and past the age of dealing with such mess,"

I said, still addressing the radio, and flipped over to the easy listening station.

At forty-nine, I wasn't actually ancient, but certainly old enough and experienced enough to know that when it came to the game of love, sex was at best a short-term solution to any long-term issues. Particularly when the remedy was, in most cases, one sided and service oriented. Besides, sex and I were on the outs these days. My ex got most of my libido in the divorce. Hell, truth be told, I'd actually lost that sucker somewhere around year ten. And then, whatever smidgen I had left, radiation therapy had claimed as its own.

I didn't have time to concern myself with that now anyway. To stay on task, I started going through my mental "to do" list of every chore I needed to accomplish that day. I'm a list-maker. With list in hand, I stay organized. I feel a sense of accomplishment with every completed job. Without a list, I'm lost and ineffective. In my life, lists are a good thing.

After this delivery, I still had a million things to do before my party that evening. I was the guest of honor, well actually the twins were, and even though my friends were taking care of most of the arrangements, I had still insisted on making the cake because, well, as owner of the cake design company, Havin' Your Cake, that's what I do. All it needed was a few finishing touches. Then I still had to tidy up both the house and myself before the guests arrived. And as with most things these days, both took a lot more time than they used to. No time to dillydally.

I pulled my car into the driveway and drove what seemed like another half block around to the back. My client had left a message letting me know that nobody would be home and she'd leave the kitchen door unlocked. I opened the hatchback of my Lexis 330, slowly pulled the tray with two large, square boxes toward me, and cautiously carried it to the kitchen door.

"Hello?" I called out gingerly as I twisted the knob and pushed the door open with my foot. "Anybody here?" Greeted with the silence I was expecting, I stepped inside and over to the center island that dominated the large kitchen.

Per Mrs. Maddox's instructions, I found the rolling table designated for my latest creation, a three-dimensional pinup of Naomi's mother looking like she was kneeling on a pile of plump red pillows. The image was recreated from a photo taken when she was twenty-two with a young husband off fighting in the Korean War. I found it to be an interesting choice, as the woman was turning eighty years old today. But, hey, my job is to fulfill the client's sugar-and-spice wishes, not determine them.

Remembering my pressed schedule, I quickly assembled the cake and wiped away any excess frosting. I cleaned up the remaining debris, and with my ever-ready digital, took one last photo for my portfolio.

"Livia Charles, girl, here's to another job well the hell done," I congratulated myself with my ritual shoulder brush. I turned to leave and that's when I heard them—the muffled sounds of low moans and groans, distinctly female, coming from down the hall. Fear turned my blood cold, causing my muscles to freeze. I pushed my face in the direction of the noise, straining to hear and confirm my first reaction.

It sounded like someone was in trouble. God, was the birthday girl here? Had she fallen and couldn't get up? My impulse was to rush toward the sound and help the poor old lady out. However, the thought that kept my feet in place was the idea that the person who was in trouble might also be in the presence of the troublemaker. I'd already gone through my stint of staring death in the face. Did I really want to go through that again?

There it was again, this time comingled with a deeper, more

masculine timbre. The words were unintelligible, but the tone sounded demanding.

I stepped out of my sandals and, armed with my car key in one hand and the cordless phone in the other, tiptoed down the hall in the direction of the whimpers. I didn't have to go far before the noise became louder and more intense. It was coming from a room that, after I'd peeked through the partially open door, I took to be an office or den of some kind. Slowly, I pushed the door farther into the room, grateful that Naomi kept the hinges on her doors well oiled. I leaned in slightly and what I witnessed stole my breath and caused me to jerk back into the hallway. I collapsed against the wall and slid down the partition, placing the phone and keys at my side. Weaponry was not going to be necessary.

Somebody was getting worked over all right, and it wasn't Naomi's mother. There was a man in the room watching porn and getting off. My torso turned back toward the kitchen, but my feet had other ideas. And without my brain's consent, they headed back to the door.

I couldn't fully see him. He was seated in a high-backed, yellow leather chair, facing the opposite wall. All I could see was one golden brown, muscular thigh flexed with sexual tension. His blue jeans were pooled around his ankles and his arm made peekaboo appearances as he stroked himself into bliss.

"Yeah, lick her good," a deep, buttery voice requested. "Make that pretty pussy wet. Take those panties in your teeth and pull them. Snap 'em. Yeah, that's it. Now play with your titties. Let her know how hot she's making you."

I watched, mesmerized, as the women on the flat screen followed his every instruction. It took a second or two to realize that he'd obviously seen this movie a time or two hundred. I'd have bet I could hit the back of the chair with the phone and he wouldn't have even noticed. Those two lesbians—one choco-late, the other vanilla—had his full attention.

I'm embarrassed to admit it, but they had mine as well. In fact, in my head, I even gave them names. Coco was lying back on a cream leather couch with her long, shapely legs spread, one over the back and up the wall. All she wore was a tiny G-string and high heels with strings that laced up her legs. She had a great set of breasts, real I think, with quarter-sized, yummy brown areolas and erect nipples begging to be sucked. Her lips, pouting with pleasure with each stroke of the blonde's tongue, allowed the frequent escape of a grateful whimper. Nilla was on her knees, her apple bottom high in the air and her head between Coco's pretty brown legs. I watched as she licked the other girl's pussy through the whisper-sheer panties, getting as hot as the two of them. Well, three when you counted the guy in the yellow leather chair.

I was standing there, Vicky the voyeur, a peeping Thomasina, getting turned on by watching other people have sex. I couldn't tell which version—the real man or the Memorex women—was turning me on more. He was a stranger lost in his fantasy, plea-suring himself, and here I was intruding without his knowledge or consent. They were erotic eye candy, soft and sexy beautiful women turning each other on. All of it made me feel freakishly naughty. And I liked it.

"Yeah, touch yourself, baby. Finger your pretty pussy while you eat hers."

The sound of his deep voice, alternately shouting out orders and getting wrapped up in his own physical pleasure, added to the heat. Despite his crude language, his forceful directives stopped short of being demanding, more like requests that tee-tered between a beg and a bark, the kind that, from the right man, were impossible to deny.

Following his directions, and without conscious consent, my hands joined the party. They slid down my skirt, separating my beige, one hundred percent cotton panties from my full pubic thatch. With his voice in my ears, my eyes stayed on the screen watching Nilla suck, lick and tug Coco's clit into crazed ecstasy. I parted the hair with my middle finger, reached deep inside to find the creamy middle, lubricated my nib with my own juices, and furiously began to finger myself. As my legs began to tense with approaching orgasm, I bit my lower lip, forcing the sounds of carnal satisfaction back into my body to join the energy circling around my engorged clitoris. Judging from the sounds emanating from inside the room, the four of us participating in this secret and disjointed orgy were all about to explode. I couldn't speak for the others, but it had been so long since I'd been this hot, even longer since I'd actually had sex, that I couldn't have stopped myself had I wanted to. I came deliciously hard and silent and then leaned back against the wall, gratefully gasping for breath as my body attempted to recover.

A chorus of "YES!" singing out in soprano and dominated by a baritone, first made me smile and then forced me out of my afterglow and back into reality. I was standing in the hall of my best client's home, with my hand down my skirt, masturbating. I needed to get the hell out of there and fast. I picked up the phone and keys, quietly power-walked back into the kitchen and returned everything to its proper place. Quickly I slipped on my shoes, then hurried out the open door and into the safety of my car.

I drove about three blocks before pulling over to the curb and bursting into crazy, what-the-hell-did-I-just-do? laughter. Jasi, Suzette and Caroline were never going to believe this. Shit, I couldn't believe it myself. Then again, they'd never know, because I had no intention of telling.

My Cups Runneth Over

"Ladies, if you would all gather around, it's time to toast our guest of honor," my best friend, Jasi Westfield, said, taking over the proceedings.

"This is her place, so technically, she's the *hostess* of honor," I heard my other best friend, Suzette Amburo, interject, to which my other BFF, Caroline Bluth, added, "Guest or hostess, it really doesn't matter because it's the girls we came to see."

From on high, I tried to swallow my laughter. My successful reconstructive surgery was the reason my friends were gathered downstairs for this oglefest. The theme, *My Cups Runneth Over*, was smart-aleck Jasi's brainchild, and as I had quickly pointed out, a bit of an exaggeration. My cups do not run over because I chose perfect, Goldilocks breasts: not too big, not too small; just right 36Cs, to be exact. It was a one-cup upgrade, but I figured since gravity was no longer an issue, why not go for the gusto?

It was actually Suzette's idea to throw a party to properly introduce my new breasts to the rest of the group. And even though I kept insisting that they didn't need a full-out debut, I'm glad she didn't listen to me because the long and winding road leading up to this happy day had been paved with woe and tears.

We all deserved to celebrate because while we might have been lighthearted and joking about it now, things had been a lot scarier last year. During my annual mammogram, my doctor discovered I had stage-one breast cancer. But after two lumpectomies and accompanying rounds of radiation, the cancer still wasn't gone, so I elected to have a double mastectomy and be done with it.

Three months before the party, I had reconstructive surgery, and tonight I was alive and well and standing at the top of my staircase dressed in a boob-busting outfit that put the sin in sensuality. It was so not me, being a woman whose daily uniform consists of jeans and white silk tops of varying styles, but Jasi had insisted the attire went with the theme. And that night, after my afternoon of unintentional, mind-blowing self-service, it definitely fit my mood.

"Ladies, raise your glasses to Livia Charles and the twins, Boobie and Licious!" Jasi called out.

Apparently having a friend with cancer makes one crazy.

I heard my musical cue, the tacky beat of a stripper's snare drum (another of Jasi's bright ideas), sucked in my cheeks and stomach and started my sorry interpretation of the supermodel walk—that awkward pony strut that Naomi Campbell makes look so ridiculously sexy. With my counterfeit golden gait, I proudly sashayed my nubile young breasts, followed by my much less perky, almost-fifty behind, into the roomful of nine cheering friends.

"Well, isn't she a showboating fool today," Caroline chimed in, laughing as I made my descent. "You're awfully frisky tonight, Missy."

"Yes, she is. Did you get some today? Did you already break in the girls?" Jasi called out.

Through the catcalls, whistles and applause, I managed to get down the stairs and into the living room without tripping. I did a couple of runway turns and then fell to the couch with a burst of laughter. Immediately, the women pounced. I had more fingers and hands poking and prodding my breasts than a stripper at a bachelor party. The consensus was that the twins not only looked great, but felt close enough to the genuine thing for me to be immensely proud of them.

"Time for gifts," Suzette announced as she led me over to my appointed guest-of-honor chair and proceeded to further embarrass me by tying a pink bra under my chin. The cups were decorated with streamers and ribbons and formed twin peaks on my head. I looked like some kind of sorry medieval advertisement for Victoria's Secret. I left it on long enough for them to take blackmail pictures, and then, amid a chorus of boos, removed it and stuffed it under the chair.

Did I mention that I am not spotlight material?

"We felt the girls needed adornment," Jasi declared before handing me a small black gift bag.

I reached in, shaking my head in anticipation of the sick joke I knew awaited me. Crazy Jasi did not disappoint. To her delight and that of my other twisted friends, I pulled from the bag a pair of red tasseled pasties and matching sheer red thong.

"If you're going to have stripper boobs, you need the right outfit," she said, amid everyone's laughter.

Moving on....

Suzette's gift was a racy demi-cup concoction of sheer black lace adorned with pink bows. For the next fifteen minutes, I opened box after box containing beautiful bras (and most included matching panties) of varying styles, colors and fabrics but with one recurring theme—all were the extreme opposite of the sensible basics that currently occupied my lingerie drawer, the sexier the better.

"Game time," Jasi announced as Caroline and Suzette cleared away my gifts and brought out a fresh round of my favorite cocktail—rosé champagne.

I groaned as I accepted pen and paper with a wry smile. This was bound to be interesting if not totally embarrassing.

"Okay, Livi, pick one from each pair. Lucy or Ethel. Polish or Italian. Leather or lace. Battery or solar. Brangelina or Tomkat."

I wrote. The others drank and watched.

"Okay, now answer these," Jasi continued. "The room I hate to clean most is *blank,* and why? My favorite place to shop is…? And lastly, pick one: Beyoncé or Jay-Z?"

I quickly jotted down my answers with little consideration. Better to get this over with as fast as possible than dally over an answer that in the long run didn't really matter.

"Now let's see what we've learned about our lovely Livi," Caroline said, taking my answers. "I'll just substitute a few words here and there to make things more interesting.

"Hello, my name is Livia. You've met the twins, Boobie and Licious, and now I'd like to introduce, Ethel," she said while Jasi gave my crotch the game-show girl, double hand point.

The female roar rivaled that of a Denzel sighting. I cringed. First of all, anyone who knew me would know I'd never name my body parts, especially my vagina. That was like putting clothes on a dog—cute but pointless. And secondly, if I were to name it, you could bet it wouldn't be a moniker that sounded like Grandma's coochie.

Caroline continued.

"My 'sausage' of choice is Polish because Ethel likes her kielbasas big and wrapped in lace. I prefer my sex toys solar operated, and the idea of a threesome with Brangelina turns me on. I hate having sex in the bathroom because it's messy and you have to do it every week, but I'd love to lick Beyoncé's ice-cream cone while Jay-Z watches."

This time the spontaneous tingle in my panties caused me to smile. Caroline's joke brought the hot thrill of my pseudo–group sex scene rushing back into my mind. For a hot second, Coco and Beyoncé were one. I felt the release of arousal and crossed my legs to stop the wet heat from spreading through my body. This was all too confusing. I am definitely a hundred percent penis girl, but ever since today's matinee, girl-on-girl action topped the hot meter. The flush must have showed on my face because the next thing I knew, Jasi was calling me out.

"Livia, are you okay? Looks like the thought of tasting Beyoncé's ice cream has you all hot and bothered. Look at her smiling. Livi, are you turned on?"

More teasing howls. I buried my head in my hands. Yes, it was a joke, but talking about my sex life in public was embarrassing. Hell, the ex and I had rarely talked about it in private. That's why I'd decided not to tell Suzette, Jasi and Caroline about what had happened that afternoon. I didn't want to be teased about it or have it come up at some inappropriate time. I wanted to keep it private, my own delicious secret that I could pull up and savor in the privacy of my own fantasies.

"Move on," I insisted, blaming my pinkish tint on the champagne.

"Livia, you are such a prude," Suzette teased. "Don't you dare waste that fabulous new rack of yours on baking cupcakes day and night. Promise you will take the twins out on lots of playdates."

"In other words, it's time for you to really do the whole *la dolce vita* thing," Jasi chimed in. "And that includes taking your no-sex-havin' self out to the club and getting into all kinds of yummy trouble. I'll bet you've never had a one-night stand, have you?"

I shot her my practiced, slit-eyed, *you're-kidding-me, right?* look.

"Come on, Jasi, Livia doesn't even own a vibrator. Do you think she's going to have sex with a man she just met?" Suzette asked.

"When and where does she meet any men? She's always up to her armpits in flour. We have to start her off slow," Caroline added.

"You need a fuck-it list," Jasi announced.

"A what?" I asked for all of us.

"A fuck-it list—like a bucket list—but instead of being about sky diving or climbing Mt. Everest before you die, it's a list of all the sex stuff you'd like to try before your pussy dries up," Jasi explained.

The squeal of approval nearly shattered my chandelier.

"Girl, let those fabulous hooters be the start of a new, sexy, sensual you. Promise that before your next birthday, you'll put on one of those pretty new bras you just got and let some sexy, handsome stranger peel it off of you while the night is still young and the bubbly still cold."

"That's right. Preach, Jasi," Caroline said as she stuck out her left hand and crooked her little finger. The blue diamond ring that she, Suzette, Jasi and I all bought and wore as a sign of our lifelong friendship sparkled in the light. "Pinky swear right now in front of all the women here whom you love and who love you back, that before your fiftieth birthday rolls around, you will have compiled your fuck-it list with at least ten entries of those deep, dark sexual fantasies you keep safely locked up in your imagination, and made them come true."

"Ten?" I asked in open-mouthed disbelief.

"Let's get real," Suzanne interrupted. "Make a list of ten and fulfill at least one."

I hesitated. We were all pretty serious about the pinky swear. Once given, there was no taking it back. I took in a deep breath and let out a noisy exhale before extending my hand. Nervous excitement bubbled up from my toes and through my body causing a wide but shaky smile to break out across my face.

What the hell! Cancer makes you bold, right? Plus, in reality I'd already fulfilled my promise. None of these women could argue that getting off in the hallway of a stranger's house while watching a sexy thigh in a yellow leather chair masturbate to the celluloid sight of an interracial couple of lesbians did not qualify as a genuine act of sexual outrageousness. Knowing I had them beat, I laughed aloud, reached out and hooked my diamond-encircled little finger into Caroline's.

"I swear that within the next six months I will find some, as Jasi says, yummy trouble to get into."

"To Livia!" Jasi exclaimed as everyone picked up her champagne flute, "as she works to find her inner freak."

I raised my glass with the others, annoyed that I now had to do something to fulfill my promise, when I already knew that my inner freak did indeed exist. Two questions remained, however. One, could I coax her out again or had she packed up her marbles and gone home for good? And two, did I even want to come out and play again?

The Fuck-It List

Suzette, Jasi and Caroline had done such a great job of cleaning up after the party that there was nothing left for me to do but pour myself another glass of champagne, gather up my lacy loot and take myself upstairs to unwind. This had been a crazy-ass day and I needed some quiet time to wrap my mind around everything that had happened. I wanted to review (and revel in a little bit) my behavior at my client's home, but the echo of female voices filled my head with an incessant barrage of unsolicited commentary.

You're such a prude...your no-sex-havin' self...yummy trouble...one-night stand...doesn't even own a vibrator...start her slow...you're such a prude...prude...prude...

Wait a minute. Prudes don't do what you did this afternoon, a voice from deep down within chimed in.

Ignoring the voice, I slipped out of my rhinestone-encrusted halter dress and into Jenny's gift of a velvet balcony bra. And in yet another atypical move, I padded over to the mirror for a head-to-toe inspection. For me, the large mirror was merely a feng shui decorating move. I never looked at myself in a full-length mirror with more than a passing glance while fully dressed, so standing in front of one seminude was a rare happening, and doing so completely in the buff a non event.

But tonight I wanted to see...well, me.

Even knocking on the door of my fifth decade, the demigods in charge of aging had been kind. My face was relatively unlined and despite a few little age spots around my eyes and a couple of pores on my nose that you could plant tulips in, it kept secret my true age. Every feature of my youth—my pouty mouth, pug nose and almond-shaped brown eyes—still hung together in a pleasing, deserves-a-second-look mosaic and now their collective beauty was highlighted by the wise glow that comes with life experience. My shoulder-length hair, still untainted by gray, was full of healthy layers that framed my face like mahogany fingers.

I did a slow pirouette in the mirror. Dressed as I was in a hot bra and my usual Fruit of the Loom granny panties, the visual before me was definitely a tale of two biddies: hot chick versus old babe. A classic good news, bad news scenario. The good news was my bust, which, showcased in this up-and-at-'em, fuchsia-colored bra, was freakin' spectacular. The new girls were perky and upright, and because I had the best plastic surgeon on earth, looked totally natural and not like someone had super-glued half a cantaloupe on each side of my chest.

The bad news was also my bust. This set of knockers looked out of place on the rest of my nearly half-a-century-old body. My new boobs were now part of a premenopausal, size-eight torso that on any given day fluctuated to a size ten just because it felt like it. I dropped my drawers to the floor, turned to inspect the rear view and cringed. From the front, I was a hottie; from the back, a total nottie. My breasts no longer drooped, but my cellulite-kissed butt sure did. Definitely too much time had been spent taste-testing cake batter and not enough doing crunches.

Note to self, I thought, *add a gym membership to your "fifty and fabulous" birthday list.*

I was soft. A comfortable, rumpled bed at the end of a hard day kind of soft, but soft nonetheless. But you know what? My friends didn't lie. I was still kind of sexy. And as a compliment, I blew myself a coy and campy kiss, which made me laugh. And then for some unexplainable reason, I started imitating the looks of erotic bliss I'd seen this morning on the wall of Naomi Maddox's den. I slowly licked my top lip like I'd seen Coco do and released a seductive *ooh*. I closed my eyes and with open, welcoming lips, let my head fall back with an aroused moan just like Nilla had done while Coco had sucked her nipples. Before I knew it, I was in the throes of a hot and heavy *When Harry Met Sally* meets *Debbie Does Dallas* display of faux-orgasmic delight. Feeling silly and spent, I climbed back in bed, confused by my feelings.

The orgasm might have been fake, but the desire it stirred up in me definitely was not. I was horny. Again. Still. And not just your run-of-the-mill horny, I'm talking Maxwell, "Til the Police Come Knocking" horny. Barry White, "Deeper and Deeper" horny. I was craving sex tonight more strongly than I had ever craved it before in all of my copulatory life. And this wasn't longing that stemmed from two years of mere lack. This was different, more raw, more urgent; less quick fix and more long-term satisfaction kind of desire.

You had sex for years but never with any real passion, my inner diva announced.

Jasi and the girls were right about me. I was a no-sex-havin' so-and-so whose vagina should be named Ethel for all the action she got. But I didn't want to be an Ethel anymore. I wanted to feel hot and sexy now and always, just like I had all day after bringing myself to orgasm within earshot of a stranger. I wanted a bold, confident, bad-girl vagina. A vagina named Suzy, Lola or Sadie—a vagina that was powerful and sexual and knew what it wanted and took it.

Start with the fuck-it list, I decided. A list that would fulfill my promise to my girlfriends and at the same time set my inhibitions free.

Purposefully, I sashayed down the hall to my office and sat Ethel down. From the drawer, I pulled out the pink-and-black flocked journal Caroline had given me for Christmas. It seemed an appropriate journal for this particular inventory. I thought for a moment and quickly realized that first things being first, I needed to make two lists—both personal, but one more defining than the other. I pondered for a bit and then, under the heading of *Livia's Sexy Sidekick,* added names that in one word, exuded sensuality and sexiness.

Livia's Sexy Sidekick
1. Lola
2. Tina
3. Suzy
4. Quincy
5. Trixie
6. Sophia

Lola I liked a lot. I thought of the song, "Whatever Lola Wants," and while partial to the message, it sounded way too cliché, so I eliminated her. Tina, my inspiration being the incredibly sexy and timeless Ms. Turner, didn't quite do it either. I didn't have that raw, smoky sensuality and no matter how hard I tried, never would. Suzy sounded way too sexy girl next door. Trixie was too "The Honeymooners," and Sophia, while it conjured up the hot, *molto* sexy Italian legend, sounded too sophisticated for me. I needed a handle that, when called, felt familiar, but spoke to a different part of me. The sexy, adventurous part of me.

It took me twenty minutes, but after careful consideration, my vagina had a first name—it was Q-U-I-N-C-Y, and I had a whole new attitude. Quincy sounded like a modern, fun, adventurous and mischievous lover. Everything I desired to be.

It was getting late, but I wasn't sleepy. I decided to move my required list-making task to the bathtub. I drew a warm bath, adding green tea–scented bath salts to the water. The hot water, mixed with the salts, released a calming, steady stream of earthy smelling scent into the air. With candles ablaze, Michael Bublé singing in the background and a fresh flute of champagne sitting on the edge, I sat back and relaxed into the water, surrendering my hang-ups and unleashing my imagination for the task ahead.

Drying my hands and picking up my journal, I titled this list: *What Would Quincy Do?* But once that was done, I had no idea where to start. I quickly drained the glass of champagne and let the buzz go to my head to pry loose whatever sexual fantasies were there hiding behind a lifetime of appropriate and ladylike behavior.

I thought about conversations I'd had about sex with my friends, about sex scenes in movies and books that I'd enjoyed and that had turned me on. Fueled by champagne and pent-up frustrations, I let that inspiration move my pen. And before I knew it, Quincy had quite a fuck-it list awaiting her.

There were nine action items on my WWQD list, and one

to go, but the now tepid bathwater was killing my champagne buzz and slowing the creative flow. I put the journal down and turned on the hot water, making a sensual game out of directing the warm water over my shoulders and bosom. The strong cravings I'd felt earlier, strengthened by my concentration on erotic ideas, were back with a vengeance. I needed relief. And with no man in sight, that left the job up to me.

With Michael Bublé's sexy Rat Pack voice begging me to tell him, "*Quando, Quando, Quando,*" (when, when, when) in the background, I reached for the bottle of sesame body oil. I tipped it slightly over my body, letting the warm oil drizzle down the full and fleshy mounds on my chest. For the first time since my surgery, I manually inspected my breasts with carnal intent, experiencing their nubile firmness with proud excitement. Did my natural set ever feel this firm or look this sexy? No longer incubators of disease, they were brand-new and more-lethal-than-ever weapons of mass seduction. And for the first time, they felt like a true part of me. As the earthy scent seduced my nasal passages, I cupped my breasts with both hands, gently pushed them together and watched as one thick fragrant drop traveled down my left breast and hung clinging to its tip. I captured the drop on my fingertip and slowly massaged it into the nipple, feeling the slightest bit of sensation. I pinched harder, applying more pressure as they began to swell under the slippery smoothness of my oily fingers. They were definitely not uber-sensitive as they'd been before surgery, but in my book, any sensation at all was a good thing.

My nipples erect and my head full of erotic possibilities, I was overcome by a rush of steamy desire that had nothing to do with sitting in a bathtub full of hot water. I closed my eyes and slipped effortlessly into my fantasy. I was back at Naomi Maddox's house, but this time I was inside the room and sitting in the tall, yellow leather chair. He was naked and sitting across from me on the footstool. The man my mind created was fine, friendly and vaguely familiar. He had Terrence Howard's bedroom eyes, Denzel's charismatic smile, and the Rock's hard, chiseled body: a DNA bonanza of Hollywood features. All imagined. All good. And for all intents and purposes, all mine.

"*You want to touch them, don't you,*" *I teased, looking him straight in his hazel eyes.*

"*Yes, they're beautiful. May I? Please,*" *he begged.*

"*No. Not yet. I want you to watch me. Would you like that, baby? Would you like to see me fuck me?*" *I emphasized my query by parting my lips and placing my finger in my mouth. My digit became his penis and I erotically treated it as such. My tongue wrapped the tip in circles of bliss before my lips clamped down and, with a seductive rhythm of varied speed and pressure, sucked. I could feel the erotic pull both in my fingers and clit and I could tell that the visual, in combination with my increasingly obvious arousal, was getting to him.*

"*Yes.*" *His voice was but a deep whisper as he fought to maintain his cool. But the sight of my naked breasts, released from their satin confinement and showcased by a half-unbuttoned blouse was rendering his efforts ineffective.*

"*Okay. I promise to let you watch me but only if you abide by my rule—no touching yourself or me until I give you permission. Agreed?*"

"*Yes.*"

"*Good boy,*" *I said before treating him to the sight of me lifting my breast to meet my bended head and taking my nipple into my mouth. I circled my areola before lapping my nipple with a wide firm tongue. "You like that, huh? Me too," I told him, seduced by my own bawdy behavior.*

He said nothing, just sat licking his lips and trying to keep his hand away from his rising dick.

My vagina was wet and juicy and crying out for attention. Slowly, I did a full body stretch, shifting my weight to my feet, arching my torso away from the cool, smooth leather, and raised my skirt until it was high in my lap. Then, in a classic Sharon Stone in Basic Instinct move, I slowly separated my legs, revealing my hidden treasures, which were conveniently unfettered by fabric.

"Come closer," I commanded and watched as he obediently leaned his face into my hot crotch. I gently spread the lips of my pussy, revealing Quincy's lovely pink underside and stiffening clitoris. "Blow on it."

A steady stream of warm breath hit my wet nib tantalizing me with a fire and ice sensation and taking my desire up a notch. "Hmmm," I moaned. "Isn't she pretty? Wouldn't you like to give Quincy a kiss?"

He did, and moved to respond but I wasn't quite ready yet.

"No, keep blowing," I called out.

Back in position, he continued to blow while moving his hands, which had been clutching the sides of the ottoman, to stroke his engorged member.

"Ah-ah-ah. No touching," I decreed, painfully enforcing my own rule. Every nerve ending in my body wanted, needed, demanded that he touch me, but delayed gratification was still proving to be a powerful aphrodisiac.

"That feels nice, baby. Now taste it," I commanded, gently pulling the folds of my vagina open wider.

He dropped to his knees, and with his face directly in my pleasure zone, lapped up my creamy middle with his tongue. Wanting to make the best of this opportunity, he began to tickle my clit, first at the tip and then with the broad whole

of his tongue. I felt weak with want and grabbed his head,
pushing him deeper between my legs. Without instruction (ya
gotta love a man who thinks quickly on his knees), he began to
suck my clitoris like a pacifier, pulling the blood from the rest
of my limbs and causing it to pool at the very tip of my sexual
universe.

My hands, answering the call from a jealous chest hungry
for more attention, kneaded my breasts before concentrating
their attention on rolling my nipples until they were as stiff and
engorged as my clit.

"Stop, stop," I said pushing him away before he could make
me come. Despite the throbbing, telltale signs of an approaching orgasm, I wasn't ready to come. "Stand up."

He complied, rising to his full six feet four inches, which
placed his dick squarely in my face. I ran my fingertip against
the tender underside of his head, causing his rock-hard shaft to
bounce in my hand.

"What do you want me to do?" I asked.

"Suck it," he managed to squeak out.

"You'd like that wouldn't you? You want me to take that
pretty hard dick in my mouth and suck it until you come?"
My voice cracked. It was getting harder and harder to remain
composed.

"Yes, baby. I would. Please. Suck it. Kiss it. Touch or let me
touch it. Do anything. I can't stand it anymore!"

"Or do you want to fuck me? Would you rather I suck you
off or fuck you off?" I was getting bolder and nastier as my
arousal escalated.

"Either. Both."

"Kiss me first," I demanded, giving him permission to touch
me.

Happily he lowered his face down to mine and filled my

mouth with a hungry tongue. There was no façade of romance or love. This was a kiss fueled by pure lust. Primal desire. I loved it and it released all sense of control. I grabbed his dick and pulled it toward me. Fucking in that chair was an absolute impossibility and I damn near threw the two of us to the floor in an attempt to get him inside of me as fast as humanly possible.

"Fuck me," I demanded.

I spread my legs in welcome and he grabbed his dick with one hand and pushed it inside me. My body and mind gave a collective sigh as he glided in and out, hitting every nerve ending he could find on both the up- and downstroke. After several moments of glorious poking, he placed his hands on the floor on either side of my head in order to lift his body and adjust the angle. Once again, he began to thrust and grind with mounting intensity, this time with his dick hitting my ready-to-burst bud.

I couldn't hold it any longer. My body tensed and I heard myself scream as wave after wave of orgasmic pleasure washed over me. The release was strong and powerful and seemed to last blissfully forever. I lay back, spent and happy, feeling lost and languid in my own afterglow. A few more minutes of lollygagging and then I took a deep breath and lifted myself out of the bathtub. I quickly dried off, grabbed my journal and climbed into the bed and under the sheets.

Pen in hand, I opened my journal to finish my list, inspired by my rub-a-dub-dub-in-the-tub activity.

Quincy's Fuck-It List
1. Buy and play with toys.
2. Visit a nude beach and go skinny-dipping.
3. *Have a one-night stand with a stranger.*
4. ~~Make love with a woman.~~

4. Get a lap dance from a woman.
5. Find and fuck my first lover.
√6. Have sex in a public place.
7. Make my own porn movie.
8. Get a happy ending massage.
9. Have someone watch me make love.
10. Make love in a yellow chair.

There I had it, the WWQD fuck-it list. Giving myself a break, I checked off number six. It might have been sex with myself, but it was no doubt in a public place. Number ten was going to be the hardest to pull off, but the scene at Namoi's place had burned itself into my memory and captured my imagination. Looking it over again, I scratched making love with a woman. Like the chair, I figured adding it had everything to do with that afternoon, but I knew that while it might be the fuel of many fantasies to come, I'd never have the courage to actually do it—Quincy or no Quincy. I changed that fantasy down to a much more doable task: a lap dance.

"Who are you kidding, Livia Charles?" I challenged myself. "You are no more going to get a lap dance or have a one-night stand than Jennifer Aniston is going to get Brad back."

In actuality, the only thing I knew for sure was going to get accomplished was number one. I was going to find a sex shop, buy a few toys, spend a weekend exploring myself and my vibrator and then report back to the crew and be done with it. And while I was definitely going to do what I needed to do to rev up my sex life, I sincerely doubted that the What Would Quincy Do fuck-it list would be any more than an inventory of exciting fantasies for my bad girl to explore in my head.

And that's what Livia would do. All talk no action. With a defeated sigh, I reached over and turned out the light.

"Goodbye, Quincy. Welcome back, Ethel," I said, before punching up my pillow and flopping over on my back. As my head hit the pillow, I felt a tempting twitch between my legs—a silent but powerful tingle that spoke loud and very clear.

"I don't think so, bitch."

BUBBLE MUSIC

Toi James

The best thing about writing erotica is the residual sex. Letting your imagination branch out into all of these seductive possibilities is very sexy.

—Toi James

Gracie, here come your boyfriend."

And oh, my goodness, here he comes, switching and sashaying through the diner, heading straight for me.

I laugh, but he makes me a little nervous, this gay boy named Swan. He comes in here every day to have a large lemonade with extra sugar and a splash of vanilla extract. Truth be told, I have no earthly idea what he's doing here in the foothills of Georgia. A skinny, mocha-colored boy with arched eyebrows and a switch just isn't as safe here as he would be in Atlanta. It's weird, though; he just showed up out of nowhere three weeks ago, and he only likes to talk to me. I think sometimes that W.T.—William Taylor McDonald, my ex-husband—sent him here to spy on me, but I know for a fact that W.T. has been in jail for nearly four years for what he did to me—making me lose the baby and all—and he most certainly would never talk to a queen, much less give one money to watch me work and serve vanilla-flavored lemonade.

Swan finishes sashaying to the counter and does this dramatic, butt-first hike to sit on the stool. He puts both hands flat on the counter and smiles at me.

"Good afternoon, Swan," I say.

"Hey, girl." He picks up a menu and starts to read.

"I don't know why you even looking at the menu. You only ever order one thing, and it *ain't* on the menu."

"If I eat this greasy diner food, I'll get sick or fat—same thing. Lemonade is fat free, darling. Swan needs to keep slim and sexy for the big daddies.

I smile, a little amazed, and slide his lemonade to him. I have never met anybody like him in my whole life. Everything about him is plain out there for the whole world to see, and he doesn't care one blessed bit. I've spent most of my life locked away, and most of the people I know are the same way.

"Swan," I start to dig in, "why do you only talk to me when you come in here?"

"Darling, 'cuz you're gorgeous, just like me," he says, "and you even kind of remind me of me...when I was twelve."

"Now, what's that supposed to mean?"

"Girl, look at you." He twirls his finger at me like it's a magic wand. "You all buttoned up to the neck, hair all snatched up, and that uniform with those shoes. You look like Aunt Esther, and we all know her ugly ass ain't never got none. Girl, you a walking chastity belt!"

"Just 'cuz I don't wear my sex life on my sleeve doesn't mean—"

"Oh, please, girl! I can spot a dried-up flower a mile away, and I spotted you right through that window," he says, pointing at the storefront. "But don't worry. All hope is not lost. Swan is here." Then, he gasps and scares the life out of me. "Girl, come go hang out with me!"

He says it like it's the most important thing in the world to him. But there is no way on God's green earth that I, a born-again woman, am going to voluntarily put myself in the company of an insulting little homosexual. That's like inviting the Devil to dinner.

"I don't think so, Swan," I say, trying not to sound condescending.

He gives me a curt "Why not?" and shoots me a knowing eye. He knows why not, but he isn't taking no for an answer. "You can go with me to an art show. A little art show...at a little art gallery...with refined people like yourself," and he bats his eyelashes at me. He knows good and well why not, all right, and now he just called me out to shame me. He's a slick little thing. He knows a real lady wouldn't say no just to save face.

"When is the show?" I ask, making sure my annoyance is clear.

"On Saturday night. And don't tell me you're busy 'cuz I know you ain't. It'll be fun. Art and respectable people. Doctors and lawyers, folk like that."

"And you."

He does a double take at me, "Girl, you don't know who I am. *I* am a socialite. How do you think all these people get connected for little shindigs like this? Swan. That's how. I am a purveyor of classy social relations."

It's Saturday night, and I'm getting the feeling Swan's invitation is more community service than anything, taking thirty-something divorcées out to art shows with the social elite. He'll be here any minute, so I open the closet, where all of my "good clothes" are, and immediately remember why I haven't worn any of them in years. The clothes are expensive and beautiful, but they're textile memories of my life with W.T., and I'd just as soon burn them all right now than to put any of them on.

W.T. used to tell me I was pretty all the time. I blushed, and he knew he had me in his pocket. But seven years of being married to W.T. McDonald took a toll on that pretty. I've got dents, a jagged, seven-inch scar down the middle of my stomach, permanent bruises from where he hit me over and over—but never the face. You can hide the bruises and scars and smooth the dents with clothes, but you can't cover your woman's face in the Bible Belt without calling some serious attention to yourself, your lifestyle and your faith.

I went to college and studied anthropology for two years before W.T. found me at a Christian singles meeting. He was so smooth and good to me. And he was *fine*—a chiseled redbone with big, soft eyes. But all of that got old real quick after I said, "I do."

I should have known from the start when he convinced me to have sex out of wedlock. We had just gotten engaged and were heavy petting. All of a sudden, he whispers in my ear, "Let me feel how wet your pussy is." I told him no, that it would be breaking my vow of chastity to God, but he slid his fingers in my panties and whispered back, "Baby, in the eyes of God, we're already man and wife. Any resistance to me now would be the Devil at work trying to destroy what God has already ordained," and then he slipped his johnson right in past his fingers and popped my cherry. That was my first time.

And every time after that was baser than the time before. I've been poked in just about every hole I've got by whatever

W.T.'s imagination could think of. This "man of God" would use all kinds of nasty words to get himself off and work me up, too. It was kind of hot in the beginning, when it was just the two of us and regular old sex. We used to screw our brains out while watching the early-morning televangelists before church on Sundays, or he'd smack me on the rear end telling me I was a "bad bitch" while we did it doggy-style. And he'd always laugh in the end. But then he started to full-on beat me afterward and call me a "fucking whore" for the things *he* made me do. I was the perfect Christian wife by day, his personal slut and whipping thing by night. To seal it in his head, he used to hire prostitutes and make me have sex with them while he watched and jerked himself off. Then he'd pay her—or them—and when they left, he'd beat me bloody and call *me* the whore. He said he was beating the Devil out of me. The first time he did it was when I started to regard sex as my enemy. It had betrayed me my whole life. It was the very thing that everyone I loved told me would lead me to sin and damnation. If it wasn't my parents telling me I'd burn in Hell if I had sex before marriage, it was W.T. calling me a succubus for corrupting his godly mind with my sexual deviance. And, of course, there was the Bible—the word of God. Worst part, though, was W.T. and his angry self. Even his penis was angry. When he did it to me, it was like his johnson had monster teeth just trying to mangle me. I *hated* sex! Not much good ever came of it.

I do have one good memory of sex, though. Sort of. When I was a senior in high school, Troy Bellows, my very first real boyfriend, showed me *Deep Throat*. His idea was that he would show it to me as an instructional video so I could give him a knee-buckling, toe-curling blow job. I had considered it for about five minutes until this crazy bubble music started playing in the movie. I was laughing so hard that I couldn't even think about being sexy, much less do it. But I adored him, so I tried anyway. It wasn't very good, and the only happiness that ever came out of it was my memory of that bubble music. It got to be that whenever I had to have sex with W.T., I'd just think of the bubble music, because it was the only happy thing I had ever known about sex. That bubble music was my saving grace. It made me smile through seven years of angry, bitter sex—W.T.'s and mine. Come to think of it, I don't think I've ever had sex without bubble music playing in my head.

Even with the bubble music, we're still not friends, sex and me, and all those fancy clothes in the closet belong to the person W.T. made, not the one I want to be. I look at myself in the mirror in my panties and bra and try to imagine that woman.

The doorbell rings, and it's a good thing, too, because I'm not making a bit of progress.

I answer the door in my robe. It's Swan.

"Girl, you ain't ready yet?"

"I don't have anything to wear."

"Lead me to your wardrobe, child. Swan is here. I can make magic out of the matronly."

"My own fairy godmother," I mumble under my breath and direct him to my dresser.

After twenty minutes, Swan has found a pair of dark jeans, a fuchsia blouse, silver pumps and a light gray, silk scarf that was stuffed in my sock drawer. He pulls it all together with tasteful makeup and glossy lips to make me look Bohemian chic in springtime.

"*Finally,*" he says with all the drama of a vexed drag queen. "Darling, you look even good enough for me to fuck!"

I take that as a compliment, and we're out the door.

Swan pulls his black BMW in back of a small art gallery in a secluded area of town surrounded by dense woods. The gallery itself seems to be built into the landscape with natural woods and local rock. It's styled like a high-end log cabin with a few nude statues of gods and goddesses carved out of polished oak and granite scattered around the grounds. The place alone puts me at ease, and as weird as it sounds, knowing that Swan dressed me and is my date, makes me feel even better. I blend with the other people going in, an interesting mix of finely dressed folks getting out of luxury cars with Fulton and Cobb County license plates—professionals from around Atlanta. And the best part is that I know for certain my date is not going to try to get into my panties tonight. Swan takes my arm (like I'm his man), and we go inside.

The entrance of the gallery is enticing. Small, potted bushes of night jasmine sit at the door; their fragrance fills my head and intoxicates me with their spicy-sweetness. I can almost see their scent thicken the air and drift up the wood-planked walls covered in honey-colored shellac. Abstract sculptures undulate and curve and hug negative space like flesh and bone, and the light is so soft and warm, it feels like candlelight. A sudden tingle runs from the back of my neck down my spine and between my thighs. Angels are walking through me. For the first time in a long time, it feels good to be some place. Swan walks us up to the hostess, who is checking in guests. She's a sweet-looking girl with round cheeks, heart-shaped lips and heavy mascara, dressed all in white.

She tells us kindly, "All of our guests tonight are invited to create art pieces themselves. Supplies will be provided for you, should you decide to join in."

The thought of actually making something seems like fun to me. I smile and thank her, and Swan guides me down a small corridor. As we reach the main gallery, I can hear a few voices, but it's mostly quiet—art gallery quiet—the kind of quiet that says people are deeply pondering the pieces and whispering about what they like and hate about them. When we enter the room, I hear the words, "fuckable art" and then I see. The art pieces are free-standing men and women perched on small pedestals throughout the gallery and covered in nothing but what the Good Lord gave them. I gasp, and I guess Swan hears it.

"They are the canvases, darling. Isn't it a delicious idea?" His eyes are as big as mine, but for a very different reason. "Close your mouth, darling. Someone might think you're a prude."

I have never felt like such a prude in all my life. I am THE prude. I was raised to be a prude. I don't know how to be anything but a prude. All of the "canvases"—about twenty men and women of all shapes, sizes and colors—stand in neutral positions with their hands at their sides, waiting for their artists to transform them into "art." While a few budding artists dive right in, most people stare in amazement with dirty little grins on their faces. Others pretend like they don't even see them, and instead talk to each other about the inanimate works dotted around the gallery. But it's all sex—photographs, sculptures, framed poetry—and milling around are stark-naked waiters and waitresses carrying flutes of champagne. (I'm sorry, but the black bow ties around their necks just don't count as a uniform.) A striking woman walks up to a female canvas, gently brushes the hair off her shoulder, and lets her hands fall down the curves of the canvas's teardrop breasts and the hourglass of her waist and hips. My fingertips start to sweat. I raise my hand for a waiter's attention.

Swan comes to my rescue with an equally sweaty glass of champagne. I'm not much of a drinker, but Jesus drank wine, and well, desperate times call for desperate measures. I take a hearty swig, and Swan leads me toward a man-canvas. At first, I can't see anything but his nakedness. His skin looks like red clay mixed with dark chocolate; it's both dark and bright with fire at the same time. I try to look at his eyes, but I can't turn away from the flame in his skin. Then a chorus of angels flows through me, and this time, they stay between my thighs to frolic with my yani-girl for a while. I give her a gentle squeeze. It feels good. I close my eyes and lick the remaining bubbles of champagne from my lips. My mind is starting to get sudsy. When I open my eyes, I realize the man-canvas is about six feet tall. His chest is toned but not too muscular. His stomach is flat and defined but not "cut." I glance down below his stomach, and…oh, my goodness! I keep going to his thighs and then his calves. Even when he's standing still and relaxed, I can see the contours of his muscles. He isn't just perfect; he's a god!

"Gracie, this is Barrett Gold. He's a friend of mine."

When I turn to Swan, my face flushes hot. He sucks his teeth at my blushing and sighs.

"Barrett, don't mind her. She's just hard up 'cuz she ain't had no dick in a long time, and you the first real man she's seen in years, and she don't know how the hell to act around a naked man, especially one as fine as you. Barrett, this is Gracie. She's my friend, too."

What kind of introduction was that? My heart drops into my stomach. But before I can react, Swan shoves a hand caddy full of body paints and brushes into my arms and makes a grand bow.

"Now, if you will excuse me, I think I see me a new papa bear in search of a beautiful cocoa twink, and you both know I am made to fill *that* order!" And he saunters off just like that. No apology; no nothing, just an embarrassment and good-bye. I can't stand him!

After that introduction, all I want to do is run away like a schoolgirl. I look down at the caddy in my arms, and as if he knew what I was thinking, Barrett says, "Don't go yet."

I smile a nervous smile. "I don't know what's wrong with him. I have to make a mental note to find a friend with a filter."

"Oh, he's all right. That's why he brought you here. Tonight is not about filters. It's about what you would do if you had no filters."

"He told you about me?"

"Only that this show is what you needed. He said you were—"

"Uptight," I huff.

"'Closed up' is what he said. He wants you to open up, so, he reserved me for you."

I glance over at Swan running his finger across some old, fat man's chest, and I shoot daggers at him. I turn back to Barrett. "And you think you've got what it takes to open me up?"

"Gracie," he says, slipping submission into the sex in his voice, "it will be my absolute pleasure to try."

I take a swig of champagne. "I don't know what to do...with you...I mean, here. I mean—" I shake my head and close my eyes, hoping for a do-over.

He saves me. "Well, you can pose me any way you like and paint me any way you like." His voice deepens with an air of naughty professionalism. "You can touch me anywhere you like. I'm your subject, your model, your canvas. While we're here, I'm yours for you to do with whatever you think is beautiful."

"Do you have any clothes?" I wince, already knowing the answer.

"No. I'm sorry, I don't have any available for you."

"Why?" My curiosity speaks before me. "I mean, what makes somebody want to stand naked in front of a room full of people?"

"It's a long story, but the short version is, I'm curious. People kind of lose their minds when it comes to sex. The body and mind want to do so many creative things, but there are all of these rules. 'Do not,' 'Thou shalt not,' 'Restricted,' 'Prohibited.' The only rule should be consent. I just want to see what people will do in a space where it's okay to let their imaginations run wild." Then he leans in and whispers in my ear. "What's going through your mind, Gracie?"

My yani warms and loosens. I have a flash of vision and almost feel him moving inside me. I take the last gulp of champagne from the flute and let the bubbles work their magic.

I sit the caddy down on the floor and walk around him to see what I'm working with. He's just as perfect on the back side as he is on the front. I look at the muscles in his back and how they dip and rise and roll from left to right when he moves. The small of his back curves down and out to the most perfect roundness I have ever seen. It's full and tight and caves in at the sides. I want to touch him right there, but it's too much for me. I just might kiss the spot. My heart is pounding so hard I can hear it in my ears and pulsing against the band of my panties. I squeeze my yani one more time. My toes tingle, and I feel my panties get warm and sticky.

"You know, God made rules for a reason," I say.

"Then God shouldn't have given us imaginations and free will."

Dang it! I'm out of champagne.

I look around for the waiter and see the spirit of the show has set in. Most people are finger-painting to create their "art." Men are coloring breasts, caressing nipples to make them—and themselves—grow hard. One man has decorated a woman-canvas, who has an enormous, round bosom, as an elaborate dessert with two giant penises as the "bananas" on either side of her, the butts of two other canvases bent over her as the ice cream scoops, and her plump breasts portrayed as giant, glittery gumdrops. For a splash of color, the artist has placed huge cherries on the "scoops" and between her legs, and then he starts stroking himself in order to add the cream to top it all off. The less imaginative are cutting designs into pubic hair. Some other folks are erecting sculptures out of penises that curve this way or that. A few of the guests have taken off their own clothes and are painting each other. A couple in the corner is now naked and literally bringing to life the Kama Sutra photo above them. The temperature in the room has gone up twenty degrees, and I'm starting to sweat. I snatch the scarf from around my neck and fan myself with my shirt. I reach into my caddy and pull out a paintbrush—the longest one I can find.

I dip the brush into some black paint, and as I reach out for my canvas's chest, my hand is trembling. Breaking all of the rules of a good canvas, Barrett gently takes my hand. His touch startles me. I like to think it's because of his sudden movement, but I know that isn't it. I jumped because he scares me to death. In five minutes, he's got me thinking and feeling things that go against everything I know to be right and true and safe. I try to pull it together, but then he takes my other hand and puts it on his face. He closes his eyes and turns his head to smell the perfume on my wrist. It's one of my spots, and a hot rush swells my yani walls. I lean forward to smell him, just him. He's been chewing spearmint leaves, and his skin is slightly musky. I bathe myself in his scent as it floats out and wraps itself around me, cradles me and rocks me. I can feel the wetness building up in my panties, and I glance back at the Kama Sutra corner, wishing I was there with him. He lets go of my hand, and I look down at it. It has stopped shaking, but it is just as wet as every other part of me.

"Thank you," I say.

I breathe one good breath and begin again. I position his

body in the form of a matador taunting his bull, pour red paint into my hand and begin to create. I start with his chest and move across the contours of his body, all of the peaks and valleys of him, the firmness of where he is flexed and the softness of where he is relaxed, the bones in his feet, and the veins that connect everything. Nothing else matters right now except for him. When I think I'm done, I realize thirty minutes have gone by, and I step back to see what I have done. I've detailed him with bright, abstract designs over most of his body—a painted pony—but when I scan his entire body, I see there is one part of him that is noticeably unpainted, untouched by my hand. I laugh at how ridiculous he looks and how stupid I must look as his artist. I look him in the eye, then drop my gaze. Jesus, it's a prize!

"Anywhere?" I try to contain my own dirty little smile.

"Anywhere." There is no smile on his face. And this time, *he* glances at the corner.

I ratchet my brain to refocus. I have been so brave up to this moment, I decide to go for it and bend down to face my fear. The champagne is gone, but here they come anyway—*the bubbles— happily popping like a kid blowing into milk through a straw. Pop, pop, pop! Then the raunchy, porn synthesizers bown- chika-wown-wown in the background...and then the melodic horns.* I smile with the sound of bubble music in my head, let some gold paint trickle across my fingers, and take my canvas's penis into my hand. It's long and fleshy-soft, but as I begin to apply pressure with my hand and rub the warm, slick gold all over his shaft, I can feel my canvas come alive, inch by inch, in my hands. The harder he gets, the harder my clit gets and it sends little shocks of electricity through me. I imagine him taking it in his mouth and giving it a little tug just to drive me crazy. I gently run my fingers back and forth over the tip of his penis, and he flinches just a little. Just by touching the smooth roundness of his head, every nerve ending inside me is anticipating its entry into me, and my desire for it comes down and makes me wet. I open up and ready myself to take him in, all at once getting looser and wetter, swelling and dripping. The rush is like a flash flood. I want him inside me so badly, I can't take it. I can't stop. I just keep painting and painting, and I can feel him getting not just harder, but swelling bigger, wider. He starts breathing hard and grunting. I know what's about to happen, and he makes no effort to stop it, right here in front of God and everybody.

Seeing him and feeling him grow in my hand like that, makes me think of what God must feel like. The joy God must have in creating us, giving us such beauty and power. He gave us these bodies to do incredible things with. He gave them shapes and feeling and colors and smells and tastes, and He didn't just give them to us for procreating. He gave them to us for *life*—all parts of it—to wonder over, to enjoy, to bask in, to feel good in. It's not evil; it's God's plan. I can see the vein in his long, thick, gilded rod pulsing. He is ready. I squeeze my yani good one time, ready for him to come, but she doesn't let go! She clamps down on just the thought of him inside me, and I come instead! I grab the back of his leg and hold on for dear life until my body stops throbbing and uncoils.

After a few seconds, I rest my forehead on his knee, breathing heavily. I could die from embarrassment right now. I look up at him and squeeze the back of his knee with my golden hand.

"I think I'm done," I say, just about panting.

"Uh." He squeezes his eyes closed, still on the razor's edge of pain and pleasure. "Are you sure?"

I feel guilty as sin for doing that to him, but I smile. "Yeah. I'm sure."

"Are you satisfied with what you've done?"

I spontaneously combust on his leg, and he asks me if I'm satisfied! My yani contracts again on her own.

I nod. "Yep, you look really good."

"Am I all finished?" he says through a deep breath.

I nod quickly.

I put my paints away and look for a getaway.

"You hum," he grunts.

"What?"

"You were humming."

I scrunch my nose like I have no idea what he is talking about. "Was I? I don't know what that was." I don't want to talk anymore; I just want to leave and get some air. I see the counter where people are returning their caddies. "It was nice to meet you," I say and scoop up all my stuff and scatter off.

I find a very tipsy Swan huddled in a corner with his big bear and pull him to the side.

"Swan, get me out of here before I'm struck down and dragged straight to Hell this very second."

"One man's Hell is another man's Heaven, darling."

"SWAN!" I want to strangle him, I'm so annoyed.

He giggles like a drunk cheerleader under the bleachers.

"Forget it. I'll find my own way home," I grumble, and I stomp off to call me a taxicab.

On Monday, I go to work as usual, but Swan doesn't show up at his regular time. I've worked myself up to be angry at him for tricking me into going to that sorry excuse for an art show with those sorry examples of "respectable people." And ME! I stayed and participated! I don't want him to show his face in this diner ever again. It would be too awkward and embarrassing. Knowing him, he'd say something, and I'd wind up telling him that I can't get Barrett out of my mind. I can't shake the feelings he stirred in me. They're so strong that not even my accidental orgasm could make them go away. I've been carrying around extra panty shields for two days just to keep dry. He tricked me into going against everything I believe in regarding sex and seduction, just like a devil would. Swan is the Devil, and he'd better not come swishing back in here or I'll spit in his lemonade and sic Jesus on him!

I start putting in breakfast orders and then the bell above the door tinkles. All I hear is Tammy say, "Jesus Christ," in a "this-is-serious-Jesus-Christ" kind of way. I turn around, and Barrett Gold is standing at the counter holding a bunch of spectacular flowers. He's wearing jeans and a white T-shirt, white against the fire of his brown skin. I'm too stunned for words, so I just sop him up with my eyes.

"Swan said I could find you here," he says smoothly.

Emissary of the Devil.

"So, what, he sent you to butter me up?"

"Yes. And I wanted to apologize to you, too." He slides the flowers across the counter to me. They're unusual. Not your typical roses, but a cluster of white orchids with frilly, bell-shaped lips that hang like little clitorises in a natural pot that looks kind of like a bird's nest.

"Nice," I huff skeptically. "Did he send those, too?"

"No, these are from me," he says.

"Well, I can't be bought off by some trip to the florist."

"I grew them."

"So, you're a gardener, too?"

"Landscape architect."

"A fancy gardener."

He smiles a broad, white smile, and I'm disarmed. I look at the flowers. "They're beautiful, but I don't have much of a green thumb. I'm afraid I'll kill them."

"You won't kill them. I'll teach you how to take care of them. You should come to my greenhouse, and I'll give you a lesson."

Red flags all around! "Oh, please. The last time I accepted an invitation from a virtual stranger to go somewhere, I was nearly struck blind by debauchery. Forget it. Lesson learned. You can take your plant back if you want it to live. Otherwise, consider it delivered, and tell Swan to go get his lemonade somewhere else."

He leans over the counter and motions his finger for me to lean in, too. I refuse. I just step toward him a little.

"Gracie, it's just a plant," he says.

I whisper back, "A plant that looks like a thousand little coochies!"

He cocks his head to the side. "Is that what you see?"

My eyes stretch with embarrassment.

"Maybe Swan knew what you needed all along if all you see is *pussy* in a plant."

I clench my jaws. I'm appalled!

"Gracie, no one is trying to hurt you. Not Swan, not me. I have a beautiful garden, and I want you to see it. If I could bring the whole thing to you, I would, but I can't, so I'm giving you this one rare, divine plant because it's the very best of what I have to offer you. My invitation stands. My number is on the care instructions in the soil. When *you* are ready, call me."

I'm one word away from exploding again. My lord, he's so damn fine! If he says another syllable, I'm scared I'll jump him right here on the counter. But I don't trust what I'm feeling, so I just look him dead in his eyes, looking for something wrong, some hint of insincerity, a drop of maliciousness, a glance to the left or right or wherever somebody looks when they're lying, anything. He locks onto me as tightly as I locked onto him, but it isn't hard or mean or anything that I had known so well from looking at W.T. He meant what he said. And now I'm in trouble.

"Fine," I say as if nothing had just happened, "I have to get back to work."

"Have a blessed day, Gracie." He pats the top of the counter and turns to go.

In the afternoon, I'm sitting in my apartment with my Bible open to Psalm 10:14, reminding myself of God's power so I can put things right in my life again. My eyes drift to the orchids and then to the care instruction card with Barrett's phone number on it. I keep replaying Saturday night in my head. I keep reliving the feel of his skin, his lips, his coming alive in my hands. I think about Bible study and the lessons about fornication, about Leviticus, and how I should have never allowed myself to be shamed into spending time with Swan...and my revelation about God's plan for sex.

I pick up the phone and dial.

"*Hello?*" His voice soothes me.

"Hi, it's Grace," I say, "I'd like to see your garden."

I pull up to Barrett's ranch-style house. He's standing outside to greet me, wearing cutoff jeans, a soiled T-shirt and flip-flops, holding gardening gloves. I dressed as if this was going to be an informal visit to a garden—jean skirt, white T-shirt, flat walking sandals...a demi-cut bra and lace panties.

"Hi." My voice lilts. I try to put as much apology in that one syllable as I can.

He smiles that smile. "It's good to see you. Come on back."

We walk around the outside of the house toward his backyard. When I get there, it quickly becomes clear that this is no simple backyard. It is about four acres of perfectly manicured Georgia foothill land. But trees aren't just trees; they're shaped into beautiful abstract topiaries. Hills and mounds are pedestals for sculptures. Dips and holes are koi ponds or birdbaths or fountains. There are plants and flowers everywhere as accents to structures, whatever the structure.

"Barrett, this is beautiful," I say, already glad I had come to see the garden.

"Thank you. Do you have a few hours? The garden goes back a ways."

"Yeah," I whisper, distracted by thoughts of what I could do with him over a few hours.

"We should start at the greenhouse, so I can show you how to take care of all your little coochies."

"Funny," I say sarcastically.

On the walk up to the greenhouse, Barrett is a few steps ahead of me, so the view is great the whole way. An archway of willow trees lets us out to a huge glass structure. It's just as pristine as everything else here. He's got so many plants, it looks like the Fuqua Conservatory, right down to the orchids.

He turns and peeks at me out of the corner of his eye, gives me a gentle smile. It takes my breath away, so I turn around, lift my eyes to the heavens and mouth, "Jesus, be my rock." Then something out of the back window catches my eye.

"Barrett," I say, "is that one of the statues from the art gallery?"

"A prototype. There are more in the labyrinth." The bass in his voice drips sex all over me. He's not informing me; he's inviting me.

"Labyrinth?"

"Yes, the prototype is at the entrance of the labyrinth. It goes back a little ways. Do you want to walk it?"

"I don't know. Alone with you in a maze..."

"You know, Gracie, you really don't need to be afraid of me. I tell you what, walk it by yourself. If I don't hear from you in an hour, I'll assume you're lost, and I'll come and get you. Deal?"

"All right." I'm relieved that I don't have to worry about the temptation of being alone with him, but the smile on my face is really from thinking about the two of us alone in that maze. I remember what Barrett said about sex without rules. A labyrinth sealed off from the rest of the world? I don't know what I would do without the rules, but I smile a little wider just imagining the liberation.

The labyrinth is made of dense hedges about nine feet high. There is no way to see through them, let alone take any kind of shortcut. The sculptures start out classic and tasteful in cutouts, but as I move deeper inside it, they change. Deep in the labyrinth, the sculptures masturbate and connect in ways that brought Sodom and Gomorrah down. Others look like textbook reenactments of Greek orgies. Here, though, I only see them as beautiful. I'm alone, and I'm not afraid of them. They are beautiful. Nothing in this place could be vulgar. Nothing.

After some time walking through all of this beauty, I see a glow ahead of me. It isn't just sunlight, but colorful light. I can smell it, too. It smells like the perfect blend of every fragrant plant I can think of—jasmine, roses, honeysuckle, wisteria, freesia, peonies. When I reach the center, there they all are, arranged in beautiful patterns with even more sculptures, and citrus and peach trees placed in between to balance the sweet aroma of the flowers. And all of them are being kissed by dozens of butterflies. In the middle of it all is a large water fountain in the shape of the orchid Barrett gave me. This is the center of the labyrinth, and it is the most beautiful place I've ever seen in all my life. I sit down, close my eyes and take it all in. I thank God for such beauty and lie down on the ground.

"I see you did make it after all."

I know who it is. I don't need to look. "Barrett, this place is amazing."

"It is," he says knowingly. "I brought you a blanket and some fruit."

"How did you know I'd need them?"

"When most people come here, they do exactly what you're doing right now, and they stay awhile."

I roll over, and Barrett is there with an elaborate picnic basket. He pulls out two bottles—one wine, one water—and two wineglasses. He roots around the basket and reveals a large, round peach and cuts it in half. He never once looks at me while he's doing this. He takes the pit out and offers me half. "No, thank you," I say, and he shrugs and bites into the peach. It is so ripe, I can hear both the crunch of the skin and the sound of juice squirting into his mouth. The juice runs from his lips down the center of the peach. He turns it in toward him and runs his tongue up the center to catch all of the excess juice. He is slow and deliberate with his tongue, and this time, he never takes his eyes off me while he does it. I instantly get wet and swallow hard.

I lick my lips as he takes a big and final bite of peach, and juice runs down his chin. He lets it run off, and a final drop hangs there. I grab a napkin in front of me and hand it to him. His hands are full with a glass and wine, so he sticks his chin out for me to wipe it. I move closer and dab his chin. I can smell his smell again, and it does its thing, wrapping itself around me the way it did the first time. My heart starts pounding again, and his breath quickens. I drop the napkin and let my thumb kiss his thick, soft, wet lips. He gently places his hand over mine and moves it to the back of his neck. But he waits and does nothing else. I take a deep breath and pull him in to me. I part my lips and press them against his. His lips sink into mine, between mine, around mine, and then I feel the warm wetness of his tongue searching mine. We taste each other, and my yani falls wide open.

I'm beyond wet; I have a mountain of cream rising in my panties. I want him so badly, I let all the rules fall away. I unlock all of the nasty little thoughts that make me hot and revel in them. Every part of my pussy is swollen, begging for him to enter me right this second. I lie back on the ground and let the weight of his body press me deeper into the garden floor. Barrett uses his knee to spread my legs apart and gives me a prelude with a hard, dry hump. As he unfastens my bra, I look up at the sky to see flashes of light in the clouds. Everything in the garden is more vibrant. Nothing at this moment could be more divine than the two of us becoming human all over again. We're working God's plan. I let him undress me and see all of me. I'm here with nothing on right in front of God and butterflies and birds and this man hovering over me, just looking. I pray to God that he doesn't say anything. (*Please don't say it. Don't say anything W.T. would say. Don't ruin this moment. Don't say anything.*)

He parts the lips of my drenched pussy and gently touches everything with his fingers. I remember how he grew hard and wide in my hands. I unbutton his shorts, and Good God, it's an encore! He bends to be face-to-face with me, kisses my lips—and my scar—and then runs his warm wet tongue over my clit. I immediately arch my back in anticipation of hatred, but it's not there. He takes his time with me, as if tasting swirls of caramel and pink—really eating me, really drinking me in. It feels so good, I pound the ground with my fist. "Oh, fuck!" I scream. "Fuck!" I feel W.T.'s chains give way, and my wings flutter. Fuck. It's my word now, and this is *my* fuck. Fuck. My liberation. "FUUUCK!"

Barrett works his tongue until I am so wet and so swollen,

I'm about to lose my mind, and before he can take one more stroke, I pull him up to kiss me again. In one quick motion, he rears back on his knees, pulls me on top of him and bursts into me. Like stars! I'm in the perfect position to ride him, and I do, like he's a slow bull. And while I ride, he takes each of my nipples into his mouth, one after the other, and then together. The flickers of his tongue across my nipples make my pussy pulse harder. We move together, and with each pump, I take more of everything he's giving me—longer, deeper. With each thrust, I feel something I've never felt before. It's like I'm on the edge of a cliff and about to freefall. I'm at the edge of completely losing control of myself, and all I can do is either die or fly. The feeling is coming like a wave; I can't stop it. It's coming like it's about to hurt, and I want to brace myself. It's coming. I'm coming. I let myself go with all the breath in me and fly. My entire body clinches around him, and I scream, "Oh, God!"

I hear Barrett's voice say, "God," too. "Oh, God," he repeats, out of breath.

I look down at him. For the first time, he doesn't look like he's in control of everything, and that makes me feel good. He grabs me and presses my body against the side of his face. He thrusts himself hard in me one last time and grunts, "Oh, God!"

I squeeze my walls around him one more time, and try to compare the real thing with the phantom I felt during my accident at the art gallery. I was right to come then. Barrett and I peel ourselves apart. It's getting dark. After a few minutes of catching our breath and relaxing, he goes off somewhere to light our path out of the labyrinth. But I'm in no rush. I lie here alone, half-wondering what God thinks about what I just did with Barrett. Maybe God planned for me to come here all along, and maybe, just maybe, I had it all wrong. Maybe God, not the Devil, sent Swan to me. It was the Devil who sent W.T. to mess up God's plan for me, and God sent Swan to set it right again. The Lord works in mysterious ways, but Swan as some kind of angel is just plain baffling. The bubble music makes more sense. Then, I sit bolt upright. I didn't play the bubble music! I hold my hand over my mouth to stop the scream. I NEVER had any kind of sex without the bubble music, and it didn't even cross my mind until just now. I'm struck with panic and sadness. It's like involuntarily giving up a crutch. Or worse, like losing a friend who never said good-bye. And then I think, it's a good thing; I didn't need it because there were no demons for it to shield me from. I smile under my hands and settle into myself again. Lying back on the ground, I put my hands behind my head, spread my legs up to the setting sun, and take my rightful place among all the beautiful things in the garden.

TANDEM

The Big Bamboo

Some would say, it's not the size of the boat, but the motion of the ocean. I say, who wants to ride on a dingy when they can sail on a yacht?

—The Big Bamboo

G o Sheila, it's your birthday. Go Sheila, it's your birthday," I serenaded myself in my bathroom mirror as I put the finishing touches on my makeup. My actual birthday had been eight months before, but in a "wash that man right out of my hair" cleaning frenzy, I found a gift certificate for Bliss Works, some new day spa in town. Tonya and Carmen had given it to me for my forty-second birthday and I had thanked them and promptly filed it in my junk drawer.

See, I don't do massages. The idea of a strange person rubbing all up on me gives me the heebies. The only hands I want touching me up close and personal like should belong to my man. But therein lies the problem.

He's not mine anymore. His current owner is one skanky *slore* (that would be *slutty whore*) named Debi, some five-foot-tall munchkin with huge tits that belong on an Amazon, and a weave that should have remained on the Korean woman's head who grew it. Everything about the bitch was too big and way too fake but apparently the slore was also in possession of the golden pussy. Mine was the fourth husband Debi had claimed. I'm sure he'll end up like the rest—chewed up, spit out and left for broke with his dick wagging limp between his legs. Trust, I am not brokenhearted. She can have him. Any man that would leave me for a piece of pass-around pussy needs to get the fuck out of my house and stay out. I am definitely not crushed. Just horny as fucking hell. Eight months without getting my horns trimmed is way too long for a sister who not only likes sex but needs it on the regular. That being said, recognize that I am not a ho. I'll fuck my own man till his dick falls off, but I'm not giving up nothin' outside a genuine relationship.

So while I was cleaning out my drawers (in an effort to keep my hands from going down my pants yet another time this week), I ran across my discarded gift card entitling me to a ninety-minute tandem massage, whatever the hell that was. Je-ezus. Why was shit so complicated? Whatever happened to just a regular old rubdown? How many specialty massages could they come up with to hide the fact that whether you're throwing hot rocks on somebody's back or spreading algae or some other organic shit on their skin, it's still a fucking back rub. But I *needed* to be touched by hands other than my own. Plus, Tonya kept harping on me that a good massage would help get rid of some of this damn stress that was eating away at my goodwill and making me cranky as hell. So those two facts had led me to the phone to set up today's appointment for my own specialty back rub.

* * *

"Ms. Brewson?" I looked up from my cucumber-and-straw-berry water and saw a Carlton look-alike from "Fresh Prince of Bel Air" smiling down at me. I gave him the once-over, as this was the dude that would soon have his mitts all over my back-side. He was an all-around average Joe: average height, average weight, average appearance. His chest and arms looked strong but their muscularity didn't offset his okeydokey looks. He was the kind of guy you might notice when he walked into the room but would forget about as soon as he turned around. I was safe. Judging by his looks and mannerisms, I was about 85 percent sure that this boy was gay. Yeah, I was totally safe—from Carlton and myself.

"Yes."

"Welcome to Bliss Works. I'm Carlton and I'll be your mas-seur today."

No, he did not just say his name was Carlton. I smiled broadly in an attempt to swallow my laughter. I was waiting for Will and Uncle Phil to pop out at any moment. "Great."

He handed me a warm, white terry robe. "You can disrobe in the ladies' room," he said, all proper like. Again I wanted to giggle. I mean what black man, other than the president, used the word *disrobe?* Definitely gay.

"After which, if you would please meet me in the Lotus treat-ment room. Once you come out of the bathroom it's down the hall on the right."

I wanted to say something stupid like, "Roger wilco," but instead I just nodded my head. *Let me let this poor boy alone.* Actually, I should have been relieved that it was Carlton and not Will who would be servicing me today. The way my body was feeling, it might have gotten ugly up in there.

I traipsed into the ladies' room and stripped down to my

underwear. Catching a glance of myself in the mirror, I stopped to check myself out. Shit! I don't know what that idiot husband of mine was thinking. I was a goddamn chocolate goddess: tall, muscular and firm; tight ass and tits on the small side, but still perky and totally serviceable. Not ever having had a massage before, I took off my bra and panties and threw on the robe and slippers and moseyed on down to the treatment room.

I opened the door to the Lotus room. The space was small but warm and cozy, not tight and cramped. Carlton was in the corner by a small sink pouring and mixing and I guess getting his prep on. The room smelled of lavender, courtesy of the candles illuminating the high and low spots around the room. Native American flutes and drums were humming in the background and immediately my stress level dropped from a high-octane fifteen to hovering somewhere around ten. Progress had already been made and I still had my robe on.

"I'll step out while you get settled," he said pointing to a tiny origami-looking package sitting on the massage table.

"What am I supposed to do with that?"

"They are modesty panties made from recycled materials," he replied with a straight face.

I couldn't help myself. I snorted and sputtered as I tried to hold in the laughter.

"Purely optional," he let me know as he left the room.

As soon as the door shut, I cracked up at the idea of putting on recycled paper drawers. I was sure he heard me but I couldn't help myself. All of this shit was a bit much. Fruit and vegetable water. Tandem massage. Paper modesty panties. Jeezus! I scrapped the panties. Why bother? Carlton was no threat to my naked vaginny. I slipped commando between the sheets on the table, turned on my stomach, closed my eyes and waited for my rubdown to begin.

"How you doing today?" asked a deep, accented voice dripping in sex.

I lifted my lids and found myself looking dead into the bulging crotch of a man who was definitely not the same one who'd just left the room. My eyes traveled north to find a blinding white smile traipsing across the face of a Jamaican god. I actually gulped.

"I am Benji."

"What happened to Carlton?"

"Soon come. He ran for more towels." Again, he flashed those damn perfect teeth at me, causing my kitty cat to purr.

"But what...I mean...why are you here?"

"For your massage, pretty lady."

"But I thought Carlton was my masseur."

"This is tandem massage. Like the bike..." he explained.

"Two of you? You and Carlton? Both massaging me?" Oh, now this was one hell of a specialty massage.

"Yeah, mon, you going to love it."

"Uh, Benji, is it? I should tell you that I've never done this before, well not, you know with a professional." Why I felt the need to disclose that I was a massage virgin was unclear, but it seemed like this tandem shit was something one might need experience in.

"You just relax, mon, and we rub away your worries," he promised. Damn, Benji was fiiiine and his voice conjured up white beaches, blue waters and fucking the black off of some island boy. Carlton came back into the room, giving my eyes the opportunity to take a full body scan of his partner. Let me put it this way, everything Carlton wasn't, Benji was: tall, built, dark, delicious, exotic, erotic. Oh, fuck. I was in such deep shit. The boy hadn't laid a hand on me and already my little girl dick was hard. Damn, was it too late to slip on those paper panties? At least to sop up the imminent flood.

Benji positioned himself at my feet while Carlton stayed up top near my head. I took a long, deep inhale and then exhaled for what seemed a lifetime. I'm sure they thought I was just trying to release my stress. Not even close. I was trying to dilute, displace or destroy the sexual energy coursing through my body. What had been on simmer when I walked into this joint was now cooking on high, and it was going to take everything I had to keep it from boiling over.

"Ready?" Benji asked.

"Yes," I said, deciding to just close my eyes and go with it.

It started with the simultaneous drizzle of warm oil on my right shoulder and left thigh, followed by the caress of four of the softest hands on earth. With perfectly choreographed precision, Benji and Carlton worked together to eek out every kink hiding in my stressed-out muscles.

Carlton's very capable hands worked my shoulders, gently but firmly coaxing out the stress. His touch alternated between deep and shallow and was highly effective. At the same time Benji's strong hands pressed and kneaded deep into my quadriceps and hamstrings. More oil dripped down my arm and leg as the boys changed sides, Carlton moving to my left shoulder and Benji to my right leg. They rubbed the delicious-smelling oil into my limbs working from the top down and back up again.

Goddamn, this felt good!

Their tandem touch was having its effect, and I felt myself begin to unwind and release. I was just drifting into the lull of total relaxation when the pressure rub ceased and "fingertips as feathers" brushed my inner thigh and bicep at the same time. A flash of electricity surged through the rest of my body, robbing it of its relaxed state and putting it back on alert. They continued as if they felt nothing and just when I started to settle down again, Carlton began massaging my hands and fingers as Benji took one of my feet in his hands, oiling it up and pulling and rolling each toe. For some reason, my overactive imagination wouldn't stick to the script. Instead it insisted that Benji was working over not my toes but my slicked-up nipples. Apparently my thought was my titties' command because I felt my nipples stiffen and extend like sunflowers reaching for the light.

I could not suppress the moan that escaped my lips as warm oil pooled in the small of my back and between my shoulder blades. My body felt so luxuriously sexy. Two hands traveled up my legs and came to rest on my butt, disrupting the oil and causing it to drip down the crack of my ass, while at the same time two more hands moved the oil slick south, traveling down my frame toward my waist. Carlton's torso rested over mine and I could feel his heat as his amazing hands worked their magic. Benji's were all over my ass, pushing and pulling the muscles, and though he was strictly professional, my horny mind kept imagining his hands on my ass pulling me toward what I was now convinced could only be a huge, rock-hard dick.

Holy fuck. This was as torturous as it was pleasurable. My body was feeling languid and relaxed but my libido was charged up and raring to go.

"Okay, pretty lady, time to turn over."

The two of them stepped to my right side and held the sheet up high so I could discreetly turn on the other side. I flipped over and for a split second, saw the admiration in Carlton's eyes. Okay, I was wrong. Boyfriend was definitely all hetero.

They began the exercise all over again, each taking the opposite extremity and rubbing it in all the right ways. My breath began to get shallow as their hands simultaneously brushed my breast and inner thigh. My nipples strained against the thin cotton sheet and I could feel wetness pooling between the lips of my pussy, mixing with the oil to create a sexy slip-and-slide just dying to be played with. I couldn't take this much longer. Forget the good girl. Forget fucking only in a relationship. This was a once-in-a-lifetime happening and I was going to take full FUCKING advantage.

And then opportunity knocked. Benji stepped over to the counter to get something and when he returned to the table, his dick was right near my hand. Lust is a curious bitch. Before I knew what was happening, my hand reached out and gave him a little massage of his own. Instead of stepping back in disbelief, Benji moved closer, pressing his cock into my hand. His smile shrank in scope but doubled in intensity. I turned by eyes toward Carlton, giving him a *Well, whatcha gonna do?* kind of look. Either he was going to join this party or sit it out. At this point I didn't care, but after all this slick seduction disguised as a specialty massage, somebody up in here was going to give me a happy damn ending.

Carlton *rsvp*ed by pulling the sheet from my body and devouring my "all you need is a mouthful" tit damn near whole. I must confess that the boy was as good with his mouth as he was with his hands. His tongue and teeth worked together causing my nipples to stand stiff and tall. The places he'd already worked over with his hands were now being given a masterful tongue massage. And everything he was doing up top was causing a fucking party down in my pussy. I wouldn't have been surprised if sparks were flying.

Perhaps there were, because Benji left my side to resume his position at my feet, only this time he placed them flatly on the table and parted my knees. Using his feathery touch, he concentrated all his delicious energy toward dusting my inner thighs, caressing them up and down, coming close enough to whisper across my pussy lips but stopping just short. The shit was driving me crazy and I loved it. Carlton turned his mouth to my other breast, licking its nipple to attention and then pushing my tits together and giving them a warm saliva bath. That, combined with Benji circling my clit with his thrill-seeking fingers, made my girl dick so fucking hard that it stuck out beyond my pussy lips.

"That shit is *ah sey one*, mon," Benji proclaimed in Jamaican patois as he peered in admiration. From his enthusiastic expression, I took that to mean he approved. Big-time.

While Benji continued fingering me, Carlton walked over to the sink and opened the cabinet. He returned to my side and I could smell a mix of lavender and spearmint. He rubbed the oils into my breasts before clamping each nipple with a small clothespin, pinching them hard. The sensation was a powerful mix of pain and pleasure and almost immediately my clit twitched and I erupted. I'd say a 5.3 on the dickter scale. It was nice, but who wanted just nice when this whole setup was screaming for some real nasty bitch action. Besides, my coochie needed some full-on attention. I wanted more of this tandem temptation.

"Eat my pussy," I demanded.

Benji let loose a deep chuckle. "No problem, mon," he said before muff-diving between my legs. His tongue did a lap around my fat clit. He sucked on it, pulling strong and then giving it a soothing lick. My hips bucked and I reached out and pulled his face deeper into my crotch.

"Kiss me," I requested breathlessly of Carlton. He brought his lips to mine and kissed me like he'd been doing it all his life. Damn, I'd totally underestimated the dude. Carlton might look average but his looks were way fucking deceiving. Everything he did was way above average, superior even—including kissing. Carlton's lips were as soft as his hands, his tongue just as skilled. They pressed against mine softly at first and then slipped down to pull my lower lip between his. He sucked my lip like he'd sucked my titty before sticking his tongue in my mouth and setting his kiss to music. His tongue danced with mine—a little samba, a little tango, and some straight-up hip-hop. Whatever tune he was hearing in his head was being translated with his tongue and I was loving every minute of it.

As Carlton kissed and tongued down my mouth, Benji did the same to my pussy. He used his perfect teeth to gently tug at my labia before slipping his tongue into my slit and lapping up the pussy cream. Benji stiffened his tongue and extended it to its full length and tongue-fucked me, while Carlton moved his mouth to my ears and made a happy meal of my left earlobe. He sucked and nibbled and occasionally let his erect tongue dart in and out of my ear. The tandem tongue action had my clit ready to burst, but I didn't want to let go. Not just yet. I wanted dick and lots of it.

"Fuck me, please," I begged.

"You want the big bamboo, pretty lady?"

"Yes. But Carlton first." I wasn't going to play Carlton short. Not again. I wanted to experience his brand of lovemaking as an appetizer, which, based on his massage and kissing techniques, was a combination of sensual kink. But the boy was still of average size. I wanted the big bamboo as my main course and probably dessert too. "Condoms?"

"Of course. It would be insane not to use them," Carlton replied in the same proper speaking voice that now sounded sexy as hell.

I watched Benji play with his hard dick while Carlton retrieved his wallet and pulled two rubbers from inside it. He tossed one over to Benji, who stepped aside as Carlton moved in between my legs. He dropped his pants to the floor revealing a not too shabby cock. He looked me in the eye and smiled as he rolled the rubber onto his stiff rod. Mission accomplished, he came closer, reached out and hooked his elbows around my knees and used them to pull my ass all the way to the edge of the massage table. I reached down and pulled my pussy open, holding my breath in anticipation. Carlton entered me slowly, as if to make contact with every nerve ending inside my wet and waiting vagina. Once inside, he continued to move back and forth, slowly at first and then increasing the speed with every stroke. I could see him beginning to sweat as pleasure began to take over his usually composed being.

"Oh, this shit feels good. Your pussy is tight. Oh, yeah."

I wanted to chuckle, hearing him curse like that, but it was feeling good to me too. I lifted my pelvis up to meet his, clenching my inner muscles to grab his dick on the downstroke. Benji stood in Carlton's usual spot, one hand pumping his dick and the other removing the clamps from my breasts and replacing them with his mouth.

"Oh, fuck. Oh, fuck. Oh, fuck," Carlton called out. "I'm riding this tight pussy tonight." After ten minutes of strong fucking, he let loose, bucked up against me and busted his nut. He pulled out, kissed my foot and collapsed into the chair in the corner. I was close, but I held back. Waiting. Wanting the big bamboo.

"Kiss for good luck," Benji said, thrusting his dick in my face. All night I had done nothing but receive pleasure from these two gifted men, one kiss wasn't asking too much.

I gave his knob a good slobbering. Feeling his huge dick in my mouth only served to open up my pussy wider and make the juices flow harder. Benji pulled himself away and turned me over, requesting that I get on all fours. He stood behind me and stuck his tongue in my asshole, giving me a quickie rim job. My onion ass wiggled in his face, which must have looked hella good because he stood back and let out a big groan. Benji snapped on his rubber and unlike Carlton with his slow and smooth entry, filled my hole with one powerful thrust. His dick consumed all the space in my twat, and where Carlton's fuck had been sweet and pleasurable, Benji's sex was raw and demanding. His long arms reached around to grab my titty, squeezing it like one of those damn stress balls. He fucked me long and he fucked me hard. I could hear and feel his balls slapping against my ass. The tip of his big dick teased my G-spot, turning it into a capital sensation. Each time he hit the spot, tiny tremors rippled through my pussy. His rod was thick and long enough to take care of my clit, too. I bit down on my lip, not wanting to breech the spa's tranquility by calling out the sex-driven profanities that were on the tip of my tongue.

The friction caused by Benji's hard and unrelenting strokes set off a series of shudders, escalating orgasms that pulsated and quaked bigger and harder until I exploded pussy juice all over his dick. Shit, I needed the condom to contain the cum!

My explosion was the trigger for his. His stroke went from hard to frenzied. His sweat dripped onto my ass, tickling the oversensitive nerve endings. "Take this big bamboo, girl," he roared, before squirting his load. His dick jerked and shimmied as it deposited each drop of cum into the rubber. Finally still, he pulled out of me and stepped back against the wall.

I dropped to the table and savored the sensations that my body was experiencing. The Lotus room now smelled warm and wet and totally organic—a natural blend of sex pheromones and horticulture. I had never felt better in all my adult life. Benji and Carlton had relaxed away the stress with their tandem massage and then brought me back to life with their tandem fucking. There was no part of my body that didn't feel alive—and no part rejecting the idea to return again. Soon.

IN THE SHADOW OF THE MIDNIGHT TRAIN

Cynnamon Foster

What's the sexiest part of a man? His forearm. That space between his elbow and wrist.

—Cynnamon Foster

There was no rhyme in his voice, only a rhythm that left us just short of snapping our fingers. I was paralyzed like a fly entangled in a web, unable to take my eyes off of him. And although I was not particularly fond of poetry, his words and being left me frozen in the third row.

He was visiting the university to read from and talk about his writing. James Adler was a respected poet, and there wasn't a student in the writing program who hadn't spent at least a day or two trying to figure out the meanings and inspiration behind some of his work. The department had been fussing about his arrival for weeks, but I was unimpressed and was only attending his colloquium because it was a requirement. I'd planned to daydream through it after I'd signed my name on the attendance sheet, maybe even slip out the back door if the opportunity presented itself. Previously, my idea of poetry had been limited to a psalm or two and a bad limerick. I *got* that poetry was art, but it just didn't move me. Instead, it felt like a waste of time, a dalliance, and I was at a point in my life where I had no time for such things. I couldn't dally—I was all about business.

There'd been a soft buzz in the room when he arrived. Adler strode to the front without waiting for an introduction. I was startled. He looked nothing like I'd expected. He was not a stooped, older man, as I'd imagined, with graying hair and un-fashionable reading glasses. Instead, he was tall, well over six feet, lean, and well groomed. Adler possessed a gravity, some-thing that sucked me in and held me in his orbit.

He cleared his throat and the buzz quieted. He smiled briefly, then began telling us of his *kupenda*. Until he said the word, I'd never heard it before and had no idea what it meant. Its meaning became clear to me after one line. A love sonnet tumbled from his lips, the words like butterfly kisses as they connected with my ears, caressing my cheek in anticipation of what lay ahead.

Lips like yours.

He spoke of worship and baptizing a lover's lips in a cadence that made me hold my breath in anticipation. Adler exuded dra-ma and flair in a manner that commanded that one stop and take notice, and we all did. My daydreaming never got started. I could barely move.

I shivered when he paused, and took him in. Squarish glass-es dissected his chocolate-brown face, providing an outline for his eyes. A neat goatee punctuated his chin, adding emphasis to the movement of his mouth as he spoke. He smelled good, like spice, and his scent enveloped us all without being overbearing. Adler seemed to appreciate that there was not a person in the room who was not under his spell. We were all mesmerized, breathing in time with his words, heads turning like Galilean moons, tracking his path as he paced back and forth.

This man was no amateur, and he appeared happy that he'd successfully gotten everyone's attention. At least we would all stay awake during his presentation. That was an accomplishment in itself. Most of the speakers we had to listen to left me and my colleagues barely awake and staring at the clock.

Goose bumps covered my arms and I wrapped them around my body, trying to understand what I was experiencing. His voice ebbed and flowed like soft waves. I found myself sucked in, focused on the imagery he created and if someone had looked closely, I'm sure they'd have been able to see my body swaying in response to the meter of his words.

All other sound in the room was pushed far away. Other than Adler's voice, I could only hear my own heartbeat. The poet's words had become its touchstone. He'd moved on to the next poem, also about love, but more explicit this time.

Heaven is between your legs.

My body was tense now, and I pressed my knees together as I tried to quell the familiar stirring. It had obviously been a long time for me if a few sexy words could get me riled up. But I'd promised myself that I would stay focused on school and on nothing and no one else.

Adler sipped from a glass of water and I took a breath, glancing briefly around the room. Everyone else seemed to be as mesmerized as I was. I was sweating, but it would look unscholarly if I fanned myself or wiped my brow. This was not a neighborhood coffeehouse or open mike on the wrong side of town where I was supposed to talk back. Here, I was expected to act like a sophisticated graduate student and be both attentive and respectful. I put my hands on my face, pressing my palms inward against my cheeks, as if the pressure could stop the flush. He *could* baptize me anytime.

The poet came right up to me when he was finished and shook my hand. I felt as if I were watching a film as I stared at our hands, clasped together as he pumped them up and down.

"You are—?" He raised his eyebrows as if he were amused. I could barely hear his words as he spoke to me and then ran his tongue over his generous lips.

"Geneva." I wanted to say more, but my throat had suddenly become parched and dry and the words couldn't find their way out into the open. I was too close to him, feeling almost smothered being in his space.

His wide smile seemed to hide questions I was sure I didn't want to answer. All I could muster was a slight nod before he left me standing there to move on and greet others who appeared more appreciative of his words than I. I didn't wait for the room to clear out. Instead, I pulled myself away and slipped out the back door while others gave Adler their congratulations.

The presentation had been good, but my face and body were betraying me. By the time he'd finished, the room had felt too hot and too small, certainly devoid of air-conditioning. I quickly found the faculty restroom at the end of the hall, briefly looking over my shoulder before I slipped inside and turned the lock on the door.

I dropped my briefcase onto the floor, pushing back the thought that the blue tile was certainly full of germs, and rummaged through my handbag for what I needed. I shoved my black cosmetic bag aside, moved the lipsticks and the discarded receipts that I'd neatly folded, my fingers quickly finding the comforting smoothness of an egg shape. I dragged my toy from its hiding spot in the lining of my purse, glad that I'd had the foresight to keep it in my bag for emergencies like this. Adler may have been hot, but men came with complications. My sex toy could give me what I needed and would ask for nothing in return. This was my secret weapon, one of the things that would help me stay on target and away from the entanglements that had caused me so many problems before and would surely distract me from my goal today.

My shoulders began to relax as I flipped the switch. The bullet jumped to life in my hand. I moved the safety tag to the side. *Do not insert fully into any body cavity,* it read. Hanging my purse on the hook behind the door, I lifted one leg and put my foot up on the toilet seat. I leaned back against the wall and in one movement, lifted my skirt and moved my thong to the side, quickly inserting the smooth, shiny metal deep into my already wet pussy. So much for safety warnings.

I closed my eyes and let my body grip the object inside me. My breathing sped up and became shallow as waves of pleasure washed over me. I pressed my back against the wall and let my knees press together, enjoying the vibrations. I imagined that I was with Adler and gripped my breasts as he might, massaging them gently.

He would surely play with my clit, so I rubbed myself, slowly at first, then more forcefully as the tension built. I imagined his full lips as they encircled my lips, and the probe of his tongue. He breathed on my clit first, without touching it, then gently ran his tongue over my labia. I shuddered and pressed my eyes closed tight to hold the picture in my mind. Adler flattened his tongue and pressed it hard over my entire pussy. I arched my back, raising my hips to meet his face. In my imagination, he ate my pussy good, but slowly, inching me toward my crash. He got me closer with each caress of his tongue but pulled me back each time with a rhythm that was not unlike that of his poetry. Sweat dripped down my face, and I wiped it with the back of my hand, barely remembering to stifle my moans. I was in a precarious place, practically public, and the thought that the thin wooden door wouldn't hide much added to my excitement. I was almost there.

A knock at the door interrupted my release. I managed to speak. "I'll be right out." I slid the switch on the bullet, turning it off. The hum wasn't too loud, but I couldn't be sure. There would be some interesting talk around the department if they figured out what I was doing.

I did my best to collect my belongings and make it look as if my bathroom visit had been like any other. When I opened the door, another student was waiting impatiently. She smiled with tense lips and I tried my best to return her gaze.

"You okay?" she asked. She was shifting her weight back and forth as if her need was urgent. "I didn't think you were ever coming out."

I shrugged. "When nature calls..."

I walked back to my car in slow motion, not believing that a few pretty words had affected me the way they had. I was totally thrown off, exhausted as I might have been if I'd had a long workout in the gym. Or in the bedroom.

"What did you think of Mr. Adler? Wasn't he delicious?" A fellow student waved at me as I passed.

"Delicious." I parroted her words, wanting to tell her that in my fantasy, not only was he delicious, but he was fucking fantastic as well. I wasn't supposed to be attracted to him. He was fantastic, even though he was off limits. Satisfied, she took it to mean that I was in agreement with her.

It had been Adler's being that had left me breathless, not just his words. There had been something about him that demanded others take notice. He possessed a charisma the likes of which I hadn't seen in a long while.

I needed a drink or something, obviously—more like something or, should I say, someone. It was just yesterday that I'd been walking across downtown Baltimore with my best friend, lauding my manlessness, and now I could barely breathe just imagining being with one.

The light had turned green and we'd continued on our way. "I don't need a man in my life. Not right now," I'd said.

"I hear you."

"I'm just going to be a diva, get my PhD, and I can worry about all that later."

She'd laughed. "Yup. Besides, have you seen the male students?"

"They all look like rejects from life, so they came to get educated instead. I wouldn't lay down with any of them if I had a wooden pussy." We'd laughed like I'd told the biggest joke, and it had seemed so right. Still, a few breathy words from a handsome man had left me all hot and bothered, and the throb down below challenged my self-control. Perhaps my divaness was all in my head, fabricated like the fiction I crafted and refined on a daily basis.

I looked in my rearview mirror and straightened my thick eyebrows with my index finger. I didn't have to worry though. Adler would be leaving after a few days of lecturing in the department. There would be very little time for his torture, even less time for me to get distracted. I had to look on the good side. I would be enjoying poetry more than I ever had.

"The Tonight Show" has gone off and my computer buzzed to life. The wee hours of the night were my quiet time, the time when I tried to create magic on paper, a story that I could actually sell. I'd been rejected more times than I could count, but I was still at it. I wanted my words to embrace the page and leave an impression on my reader, and I hadn't done that yet, but I was close. I could feel it.

One of my professors had said that my work was too safe. "You can't create emotion if you take the easy road," she'd said. "You have to find a way to excite your reader. Be daring. Take chances. Write your pain."

I'd shrugged off her comments. What did she know? She'd also told me to write what I know, and that is what I'd been doing, with painstaking detail, but it hadn't been good enough. My work still came back with rejection letters and sometimes with more red pen marks than a first-year writing student would get.

"What if I don't have any pain?" I'd said. That hadn't been the reply she expected. She had no answer for me, at least nothing that had moved me from this spot that I found myself in nightly. I shook off thoughts of my professor and tried to focus.

I always checked my mail first. It was part of my process, the routine I used to get started. I scrolled through the myriad of emails. Most of them were junk or spam from someone trying to sell me clothing, a remedy for a short penis, or the proposition that I had won some lottery or the other and could claim my winnings if I only sent all the money I had to some foreign locale. I chuckled. Sometimes it seemed like my odds of winning the lottery were better than my odds of getting published. I deleted the latter, and filed the messages about sales from my favorite stores in a place where I could look at them later. Online shopping would be my reward for producing at least three pages worthy of keeping. Usually, the browsing was the highlight of my day. A message from the department coordinator caught my eye. It was addressed to all of the students.

Join us for one last evening of poetry and critique with our guest, James Adler. This is your last chance to ask any question you may have. He will leave promptly at ten to catch the midnight train to the next stop on his multicity tour.

I lingered on the message, taking my time in filing it in the folder I reserved for messages from the department. Of course, I already knew that he would be speaking again. That is the way it was done with visiting lecturers, and I also knew that I was expected to be in attendance. My financial aid required me to be present at all department events, and the department head was a stickler for following the rules.

It was interesting to me that Adler was taking the train to his next stop, as opposed to flying. That said that he was a patient man, someone who liked to take his time. The feeling between my legs started again, and before I knew it, I'd been sitting at the computer, alternating between staring at that message and web-surfing for two hours. Two hours without writing a word. Two hours wasted just thinking about seeing some stranger again. So much for avoiding distraction.

I was hoping things would be better the next day, that I might have recovered from whatever spell Adler had put on me. I was wrong. When I walked into the lecture hall, he was already there. I drew in my breath as I walked by him and the four students who surrounded him, all of them in various phases of orbit, still more than enamored with Adler's presence. He glanced up when I entered, giving me a backward nod. I shivered. There was just a slight hint of a smile on his face. His lips turned slightly upward. Although he didn't move his head from facing the person who was talking to him, his eyes followed me as I walked across the room and found a seat by the open window. I let my eyes get pulled into his almost in a challenge, and I sat with my back slightly toward the wall as if I was trying to protect myself. After what seemed like too long, he finally released my gaze. I shook it off and flipped through my moleskin notebook, not seeing the words on the page, but looking for something to bring me back in, to anchor me.

Once again, I was breathless as he made his presentation. Today, he talked about his craft and answered questions. His voice still had a rhythm about it, like music, and I was trapped in its bars. My mind played games with me now and I imagined that although he spoke to the whole room, his eyes found me at the end of every exchange. It didn't make sense, but I felt as if he was talking only to me. Adler spoke, and my body hummed with need in response. The whole session seemed to last only ten minutes, even though we were there for more than an hour. The students around me gathered their things to go, and a new group surrounded him. I put my belongings together slowly, grateful that it was over. Everything felt heavy and it took extra effort for me to lift each piece and place it back inside my briefcase. I kept running his picture over and over in my head, waiting for my fog to lift.

I was glad that Adler was finally done. Now, I could get back to my routine. He would be leaving us and taking his special kind of gravity with him. A crowd of people milled around by the door, blocking my exit. I stopped to let them move aside and paused, looking back over my shoulder. He was alone now, gathering his notes to leave. I watched guiltily for a second and he looked up, catching my gaze again. Our eyes locked and his nose flared just as a hint of a smile flickered across his face. Adler glanced at the clock and then gave me that backward nod again. My breath caught in my throat. Or did he really look back at me? I wasn't sure.

I gasped, then tore myself away and slipped out the door, making a beeline for the parking lot. There was work to be done tonight. I didn't have time to sit around and exchange meaningless glances with anyone, no matter how magnetic he seemed. I reminded myself of my resolve to focus on the important things, and a flirtation was not one of them. An unwritten masterpiece was waiting.

I couldn't believe I was doing it, but I was, nonetheless, driving to the train station. I didn't know what I expected to find there or that I was even going at the right time, but I knew that Adler would be taking the midnight train out of the Baltimore County Station. I glanced at the clock on my dashboard. It wasn't even ten o'clock. I hadn't thought or spoken my intentions. In fact, I wasn't sure what they were. I felt ridiculous but I didn't turn my car around and go back to my apartment to get down to the work that was perpetually waiting for me. Instead, I kept running over our last almost-exchange in my mind.

A backward nod. An invitation. *Or maybe just a backward nod.* My inner voice had been screaming at me, but by now the more adventurous me had tied her up, gagged her and thrown her in a corner of my psyche. Adler hadn't explicitly said I should come, and if I had read between the lines incorrectly, I would look ridiculous. My gut told me I wasn't wrong, though. Adler would not complain or even accuse me of stalking. If he'd felt half of what I had, he'd be grateful to see me.

I was going against everything I believed in. Smart women just didn't approach strange men, and certainly not in a dark place at night. I knew nothing about Adler, yet I was drawn to him. A small colloquium, a normal occurrence in my daily life, had turned into such a distraction that I was sure I was doing the right thing. By forcing myself to confront him, I would be able to move on and get down to the business I needed to be taking care of. Something told me that seeing Adler one more time would get him out of my system and keep me from spending one more unproductive night paralyzed in front of the computer. I was just going to look, and that never hurt anyone.

The station was surrounded by tons of parking, a sprawling asphalt lawn punctuated by the white parking lines. As I pulled in, I angled my car away from the yellow light of the new-fangled streetlamps, to the place where the shadow of the railroad trestle obscured the light. There were only a few cars left, just as I'd hoped. Most of the commuters had already started their journey back to wherever it was they had come from for the night. I shivered, then checked to be sure that my doors were locked. My dark spot of choice was also a prime spot for me to be mugged or carjacked, but the adrenaline rushing through my veins kept me from being afraid. I parked where I could see him, but he might not be able to see me until I wanted him too.

I sat in the corner of the lot, not sure how long I might have to wait. I turned my car off and stared into my rearview mirror, watching the bottom of the massive steps that led to the platform. Three cars came and went and I searched the occupants, willing one of them to be Alder. I was as still as Lot's wife, barely breathing each time someone emerged from a car and headed up the steps. I remained frozen as I examined each person's stride, looking for Adler's familiar one. I waited thirty minutes, long enough to start to feel the beginnings of regret. Just as I was about to leave, a car pulled in that I recognized as belonging to the department head.

I couldn't even see Adler yet, but my breath caught in my throat anyway. A few seconds passed before he finally emerged from the car and headed toward the steps. I followed.

I was midway up the steps as his foot disappeared across the top step. I climbed faster, landing only on my toes, my breath coming harder at each step. As I reached the top, the white face of the large station clocked proclaimed it to be eleven o'clock.

Adler headed toward the restrooms, at the back of the platform. I didn't hesitate as I followed him, careful to avoid the shadows. I felt myself become bolder with each step. I wanted to remain visible now. I stared at Adler, my eyes boring into the back of his head as I made my way across the platform, willing him to turn around.

He rounded the corner to the men's restroom and he hesitated. Just then, he caught a glimpse of me and slowed down. I stopped and stared at him, not sure what I should say.

A few seconds ticked by, and finally, Adler smiled. I licked my lips, suddenly noticing how dry my mouth was. We stood there a second longer until Adler raised his hand, beckoning me forward with a small movement of his index finger. I glanced over my shoulder at the deserted platform, took two steps and followed him into the restroom.

We didn't speak. Adler pushed open a stall at the end of the room for me and I stepped inside. He quickly followed and locked the door behind me. I should have been afraid, but instead, my body tingled all over. It was warm, but I shivered anyway. Adler pulled me to him and I melted, allowing him to kiss me. Our lips fused together as he probed the inside of my mouth with his tongue. My insides exploded, surprising me. My reaction to his words had been strong, but my body's response was far beyond that. He smelled even better today than he had yesterday; the spice cologne he wore had undertones of vanilla.

Adler ran his hands up my thighs, lifting my skirt as he went. He squatted and put his mouth directly over my puss, blowing his hot breath through my thin, lace panties. I felt hot and cold at the same time, and I moaned, not caring who might hear. I leaned backward and gripped the sides of the stall to keep from falling.

My mouth rounded into an O and I pressed my eyes closed. Waves of pleasure pulsed through me as I pressed my pelvis against his face. He used his mouth to move my underwear to the side and began to probe me with his tongue.

I gasped and tensed my body to keep from falling as Adler drank me up. I saw sparks behind my closed eyelids. Part of me wanted him to stop. I fought the conflicting emotions and willed myself to relax and enjoy. I could feel the bumps on his tongue against my pussy lips.

He moved faster and pressed harder and waves of pleasure started at the tips of my toes. I felt a tsunami coming, rolling up from my toes, through my pelvis, then cascading outward. I moaned, then bit the edge of my lip. My body felt covered with pins and needles. I was right on the edge. Just as I thought I couldn't take it anymore, he stopped.

I gasped, whining a little. "Don't stop." I was confused. I was almost there. Was he trying to torture me on purpose?

"Shh," he said, rising to holding one finger over my mouth.

Confusion clouded my mind. Not sure what to do, I let my body take over. My panties were soaked through. Adler stood, grabbed the thin material and tore it from my hips. I opened his belt and unzipped his pants in almost one motion. They feel to his knees and I pushed him backward. His dick leaped to attention. My mouth watered in anticipation. I pulled his underwear downward and gripped his buttcheeks, pulling him to me as I bent down to return the favor.

My mouth covered him with one try. I relaxed my throat to take him in as much as possible, placing my hand at the base of his fuck-rod. He grunted as I synchronized the motion of my mouth and tongue, moving them together in a rhythm with each mouthful. I created my own metrical composition, enjoying the sounds of Adler's grunts as they punctuated the end of each phrase.

His grunt changed to a lusty groan and he pushed me away, before reaching out to keep me from falling backward. Adler gripped my thigh, and I leaned against the stall door as he hand-delivered his cock into my pussy, causing me to catch my breath. I tilted my pelvis forward to meet him and Adler let out a deep sigh and began to move upward slowly. I thrust downward, pushing him deeper. He moaned. I lifted my other leg and wrapped them both around his waist, supporting myself by wrapping my arms tightly around his shoulders and neck. Breathing came harder as he thrust himself harder and faster into me. His poetry had been just a prelude; where I felt smothered and speechless by his words before, I was consumed by his body now. The reality was ten times better than what I had imagined. I wanted to take every inch of him. My hips rose to meet his as I wrapped my legs around him tighter to draw him deeper inside me.

A slow rumbling started in my belly and my knees began to ache with pleasure. Our movements became faster and harder and I was on the very edge when an explosion made every muscle in my body tense at the same time. We moaned in unison, and everything faded to white. We didn't move. His poetry was good, mesmerizing even, but it was no match for the performance he'd just given. A smile crept across my face.

Adler had me pressed up against the stall door. As my vision started to clear, we both seemed to realize that the rumbling was continuing.

I exhaled. "Your train—"

Adler had melted into me, but he jumped to attention, pulling his penis away from me at the same time. I let my feet drop to the floor and wiped my brow with the back of my hand.

We didn't speak. Adler put himself back together so fast I almost missed it. Our eyes met, and he opened his mouth to speak. It was my turn to silence him. I closed his lips with my own and let him go.

Two minutes later, I walked past the train. I didn't turn my head to look for him as I passed. Instead, I looked straight ahead and walked purposefully out of the train station and back to my car. My good sense was returning, and words were forming in my head. I had deprived myself too much. I felt relaxed and in control and my story was already forming in my head, coming faster and smoother than it ever had before. By the time I locked the doors, the train lumbered to a start. The light from inside the train lit up the rural night. I paused for a minute to watch it pull away, then smiled to myself. My book was waiting.

TILT-A-THRILL

Noori Lun

I've never tried a strap-on, but I'd love to try and approximate what it would be like to have sex like a man.

—Noori Lun

Yesterday when I stood in line to board the tilt-a-whirl, I was embarrassed, worried that the cute but verging on jailbait ride operator would recognize me and call the police. But today, I don't give a damn. So what if I, a fifty-four-year-old woman, have been to the local fair every day since it hit town last week? So what that once again I am first in line waiting for the ride to open? It no longer matters to me that I am always alone and always the oldest rider aboard, not counting the occasional grandparent roped into escorting a child. I couldn't give a damn if they hear my screams of ecstasy or witness the look of orgasmic joy on my face.

I am here at this temporary amusement park for the fifth day in a row to do two things—eat cotton candy and get my whirl on. And frankly, it ain't nobody's business if I do.

This all happened so innocently. Last Thursday, I was forced to take a detour from the supermarket and there on a large grassy plot of land was a traveling amusement park, complete with rides and games and all the yummy, fattening food that makes carnivals so damn fun. Going to the county fair had always been a big deal in my neck of the woods. In fact, nearly every romantic first I had experienced as a teenager had happened there. My first date, with Richard Jeffries, was at the county fair. I got my first kiss on the top of the Ferris wheel, and my first gift from a boy—a pink and black teddy bear, won for me at the baseball throw. A few boyfriends later, my first intercourse-free orgasm had occurred in the fun house at the gifted hands of Warren Adams. Talk about your fun times.

I hadn't been to a fair in decades and with nothing better to do that afternoon, I decided to stop in and take a look around for old times' sake. I spent an hour riding everything from the Ferris wheel to the merry-go-round. I won myself a white poodle in the ping pong toss, had my weight guessed and my fortune told. I thoroughly enjoyed myself and decided to top off my day with some sticky sweet spun sugar. But I never made it over to the cotton candy truck. Instead I was lured by the twinkling lights and the funky sounds of Earth, Wind and Fire over to the tilt-a-whirl.

Figuring that everyone's life could use an occasional whirl, I took a seat. What happened on that ride left me sweet and sticky all right, and I've been back every day since, riding at least three times a day. They're folding up their tents today, so here I am this morning—ready to go for the gusto before this fair experience becomes another download on my memory drive.

As soon as they open for business, I buy my ticket and make

a beeline for the tilt-a-whirl, or as I've renamed it, the tilt-a-thrill. My stomach flutters with each step. Nervousness mixed with eager anticipation is a powerful cocktail especially when I know what pleasure lies ahead.

The young man takes my ticket and looks directly in my eyes. "You're back," he says with a coy half smile on his lips.

The way he smiles makes me nervous. Obviously he recognizes me but could he possibly know? Nah, I decide, calming myself. Still, he's been there every morning to collect my ticket and secure me into the car. He had to at least wonder why I kept coming back. I lower my eyes to avoid his. They come to rest on the control panel and I notice three buttons labeled ON, OFF, and JOY. I smile to myself. How very apropos.

I walk past the first four cars, choosing my favorite, number five: the magic car with the magic seat. I step into the hooded tub as usual, but this time, with a slight flip of my wrist, I discreetly raise the back of my dress before I sit down. I press my bare ass into the seat and lightly squirm, warming the cold metal with the heat of my wantonness. Within seconds, he is there, back in my face with his devilish smile, pushing the safety bar toward my lap.

"Enjoy your ride."

I swear he's laughing as he walks away. I wonder if he knows I'm sitting here about to ride this thing bareback.

My heart skips as the motor begins to grind, a telling sign that my sexy ride is about to begin. My tub, along with the six others, swings lethargically side to side as the machinery cranks up. I wait with anticipation, wondering which way my life will go spinning. That's part of the thrill of this ride—the randomness. You never know which way your tub is going to turn.

I begin to feel the familiar vibration in my seat. Like a racehorse trained to shoot the gate at the sound of the gun, my twat begins to twitter, instant-messaging the rest of my pleasure nerves that the ride is about to begin. I suck in a quick breath as my car takes its first complete go-round, causing me to slide slightly across the seat. As I predicted, the direct contact of hard and smooth metal with soft, wet arousal is raising the bar of pleasure to the next level.

My car begins to twirl, quickly increasing the vibrations and friction. I press my pelvis forward, trying to position my clitoris directly on the seat. Rewarded with a metallic kiss, I squirm as the speed increases. My stomach jumps into my chest before bouncing back, putting a pleasing pressure on my pelvic region. My adrenalin is pumping and so is the blood to my greedy nib.

One side of the platform rises, throwing my car into a counterclockwise rotation. My body shifts back to the left and my bare ass slides across the seat again. I consciously press my weight into the seat, keeping my pussy in constant contact. I gyrate and rock back and forth within the red and purple hull, savoring the vibrations that are spraying seeds of orgasmic blooms throughout my body and planting them in the garden of my sex. I move my ass in a four-corners pattern, square-dancing in place, rocking in a forward, backward, side-to-side motion. The movements are small and contained but powerfully arousing. Blood is pooling in my clit as the car shifts directions, once again moving me to the left. I close my eyes, enjoying the chaotic feel of my immediate world spinning apart, eagerly anticipating the explosion that is coming.

My stomach lurches again, forcing my eyes open. I notice that the other cars are whirling in place as mine lifts farther into the air, this time to the right, forcing my body across the seat again. I keep my hands in my lap to keep my skirt from flying up, but with my pussy in such close proximity, I want to touch it and help coax from her excited lips the powerful orgasm I know is imminent. The path twirls and undulates and the festival scene outside my pleasure ride is a blur of color and shape, adding to my sense of drunken pleasure. The boy operator stands at the perimeter of the ride platform with a direct view of the ride and riders. It is clear that he is fixated on my tub. He is watching me and rather than embarrassing, it excites me. The squeals of laughter mix with my moans and gasps to create in my head a frenetic symphony of aural sex. My clit is pulsating, ready to burst.

She demands contact. The seat, now warm and wet with pussy nectar, has ceased to supply the necessary friction to get me off. I can feel my approaching orgasm begin to ebb. I debate with myself whether to allow my hands to gratify me, fighting with the voice telling me that public displays of masturbation are lewd and unlawful. But just as I am about to give up, I hear the metallic bumps and grinds of metal hitting metal and the car begins to vibrate and shake as it tilts, changes direction and twirls in a more helter-skelter manner. Again, I press my greedy cunt into the seat and push back and forth across the slippery bench. I clinch my asscheeks tight as I let it rise and fall, and let this carnival ride turned sex toy shake, rattle and roll me into orgasm.

My screams of satisfaction mix with the joyful shouts of others and, as if on cue, the tilt-a-thrill begins to slow its roll. I lean back into the car for the first time, allowing the rippling waves of pleasure to wash over me as the tub gently rocks back and forth like a caring lover.

I take a deep breath as the safety bar releases me. My legs wobble slightly as I climb out and walk quickly toward the exit, avoiding all eyes, especially his. This has been the most powerful orgasm yet and also the only one that has left me wanting more. I teeter over to the nearest shelter, the fun house, wanting to get lost for a minute to rest and recover. Since it's still early, the enclosure is empty. Alone in my secret thoughts, I walk farther into the tent and pause in front of a mirror that distorts my body. I look like a giant—a tall and supersexed wonder woman. I may be half a century old, but I still look damn fine. I can stand next to any forty-year-old and proudly hold my own. I am shapely, sexy and best of all—seasoned. After a quick glance around to make sure I'm alone, I lift my skirt and see my magnified coochie staring back at me. She is still sensitive and greedy for more, and witnessing her in this supersized state turns me on. The temptation to touch is too great and I stand in front of the mirror with every intention of fingering myself into another orgasm.

I reach into the middle of my cave and dip into the pleasure pudding that remains. I smear my clit and begin to rub, feeling the blood come rushing back into place. I can feel it begin to grow and twitch in anticipation of another orgasm. The pleasure is so intense that I close my eyes as I rub and push, tickle and taunt my nib almost to the point of no return. It feels so fucking good that my legs buckle slightly and I step back—not into empty space as I expect, but into a soft and hard combination of obvious manhood.

My eyes shoot open and in the crazy mirror I see operator boy standing behind me, his pants and underwear pooled at his ankles. Our eyes meet in distorted recognition and with a flick of an eyebrow, I give him permission to continue.

With his hard dick pushing into my backside, he puts his hand between my legs and pushes several fingers deep into my dripping pussy. "You know, I made you come on the tilt-a-whirl," he tells me.

My eyes, full of question, look into the mirror and find his.

"I was watching you. I have been all week. I could tell you were ready to come and then something happened," he whispers in my ear as his fingers continue to investigate my innards. "So I pushed the joy button."

Again, my eyes query his remarks.

"The ride has a seven-motor system. I can single out any one car and take control," he says in a voice that spoke with amused empowerment. "The joy button kills the power to all the motors and applies the brakes to the table but not the tub…"

"Shh," I demand, his technical talk beginning to destroy my sexual buzz. The only joy button I am concerned about right now is the one between my legs. I don't understand his explanation but the fact that he's watched and somehow participated in my escapade has ratcheted up my desire. "Shut up and fuck me."

For a young man who seems to delight in being in control, he takes direction well. He puts one hand on my back, bends me forward with just the right blend of dominance and deference, and replaces his hand with his youthful, blissfully hard-as-a-metal-rod dick, and pounds my pussy doggy-style. He fucks me roughly with little finesse and all heart. Just the way I want it.

I watch in the mirror as our bodies collide with sexual force. The circus atmosphere, my uncharacteristic exhibitionism, the idea that I, a fiftysomething, widowed grandmother of two, am fucking the shit out of a young stranger, combines to create a potent stew of raw lust and hungry need. I brace myself with one hand on the mirror and push my hand under my shirt to give my breasts the attention they ache for. I pinch and roll, giving each nipple the opportunity to join the party. The direct line between my nipples and clit is still intact and I feel the electric jolt rush my pussy and cause it to pulse.

Our coupling is silent, as sex between perfect strangers often is, but the conversation taking place between our bodies is a shouting match. The sound of his pelvis slapping against my ass echoes through the fun house. The smell of sex has begun to permeate the air around us, and the aroma of arousal adds to our urgency. Operator boy begins to grunt as he gets closer to getting off. His stroke becomes faster and faster and just before he shoots his wad, he reaches around my thighs and delivers a slight slap to my engorged pussy. The surprising sting radiates throughout my pelvis and my entire body begins to convulse in orgasmic delight. He begins to buck and pulls out of me, spraying cum all over my ass. We both collapse against the mirror, our bodies still humping as the thrill of our ride slows to a stop.

Voices in the near distance interrupt our recovery. He abruptly steps away, cum dripping down both of our legs. He pulls his pants back on and is ready to head back to his job within a minute. My breath returns to normal and I stand upright, smoothing my hair, blouse and skirt. The silence continues between us, only it is awkward now. We opt to say nothing, and I am grateful. He turns and walks toward the entrance as I go in the opposite direction toward the exit. Once the sunshine hits my face again, I head toward the cotton candy truck. I receive the pink, sticky froth on a stick, smile broadly and throw my head back with a deep, satisfying chuckle. The tilt-a-thrill: another memorable county fair first.

THE ACCIDENTAL ESCORT

Erika J. Kendrick

Sexiest vacation spot? The G-spot, of course!
—Erika J. Kendrick

1

My inner thighs are wet and my lips are finally starting to tingle. *Finally.* I try to focus on the hard ribbed dick that's being thrust between my thighs. It rhythmically massages me. Yawning, I fumble around the legal briefs scattered over my laptop in search of the remote so I can mute Suze Orman.

I am tighter than normal this morning, I think, exhaling a subpar moan just loud enough that my designer cat, Jaguar, jumps from the bed. I glance at the time—SHIT! Frustrated, I grip the hard dick and peek down at my pampered puss. *Damn it, why does this always take you so long?* With only three minutes left in the five I've scheduled for my morning milk shake, I breathe in deeply, exhaling only after I feel my clit begin to pulse to the rhythm of Cash. That's Cash...my remote-control dick. I dial up his intensity, force my eyelids shut and concentrate as my fingertips find my clit.

Come on, Penny! And that's Penny...my sourpuss of a pussy that's not worth two cents. But I can't really blame her, she's been on a forced sabbatical long enough to make the best cat trap lazy. *Penny, make nice with Cash!* See, Cash is a real commodity around these parts; besides my ritual workouts with my trainer, my codependent relationship with Cash is the only intimacy Penny's been getting in nearly seven years—just long enough for me to stay focused on the grand prize and put us both in line to proudly make partner at LCA. LCA, (affectionately known to industry suits as Lights! Cameras! Action!), had quickly become one of Manhattan's most lucrative entertainment firms and I'd been working my tight tushie off for them. These days I was barely able to catch up on my sleep or even worse, squeeze in my appointment with Kiki, Gotham's double-jointed weavologist, for my routine tightening. So after putting in twelve-hour days, followed by late nights with prospective clients, I desperately needed this battery-operated release. It was quite possible that I needed it more than the five-star vacay I had my assistant book yesterday.

Ahhh, Turks & Caicos. My juices finally sizzle at the thought of the romantic getaway (even though I'd be flying solo, unless you counted Cash). *Good girl, Penny!* I am baking in the sunshine. *YES!* Stretched out under massive palm trees. *YESS!* Fanned by the glorious ocean breeze. *YESSS!* My skin snakes around the 1000-count-cotton Egyptians as my clit begins to beat louder. *Congratulations, you've made parrrtner.* I purr at the thought of the blissful words and my back bends into Cash. Thoughts of the six-figure bonus send an erotic volt surging down my spine, crashing behind my weak knees. *Right there.* Anticipation of the three-hundred-thousand-dollar bump in salary makes me moan louder. The new tax bracket meant I'd finally be able to pay off my relentless creditors and luxuriate in peace! And Suze Orman could stop yelling at me through my damn TV. My heart pumps faster. Cash is now tweaked to ten (right along with my nipples) and all I can see are Ben Franklins sun-tanning in my head.

"Cash," I whisper, gripping the sheet. A pitchy shriek escapes me. The nerve endings around my clit spark fire. "Cash!" A sweat bead trickles over my high cheekbone when I twist Cash under and around in line to my G-spot. The new BMW and the penthouse on Park awaiting my bonus push my anticipated orgasm toward euphoria. "CASHHH!" My toes curl and I cum so hard my kidneys flinch.

2

"I don't really care how much the plane tickets are running me, Reagan! This was supposed to have been handled yesterday." I whisper ardently into the Blackberry at my assistant as I clack my Louboutins across the marble floor in the foyer of my *very* white-glove building.

"But your AmEx was declined too, Ms. Stone!" Anxiously, I fumble with the row of pearls around my neck. They suddenly seem tighter.

"But that's not possible," I deny through frustration. And Denial is my arch-nemesis.

"Good morning, Ms. Stone," I hear the new doorman's tenor bellow over Reagan's mumbling.

"Uh, morning," I say, too caught up in her web of wicked words to focus.

"Allow me to get that door for you." The tall, commanding concierge moves with authoritative ease as he glides across the lobby and holds the door for me. "You look good today, Ms.

Stone," he says, polishing off the compliment with a quick review of my pencil skirt and ruffled shirt pairing.

"Are you sure?" I say into the telly at Reagan, while his
words rush between my ears.

"But I bet you always do." His sentiment begins to register
and I stop in my tracks to look up at him. Bald, with a goatee
atop supersmooth radiant skin, he towers over me—even in my
four-inch trendy stilts. Casually, he places his hand onto my
lower back to escort me to the town car. His touch shocks me
back into step. When he opens the back door, I grip the handle
on my Birkin bag and duck in. I reach for the handle but he
grabs my arms and says, "Let go; I got this."

His dimples, lodged deep in his cheeks, are accessorizing an
alluring smile, and just as I start to feel my cheeks flush, he
bends down and whispers, "Now, make sure you have a good
day." I feel my lips tremble as he closes the door. I watch him
turn to walk away and am shaken from my gaze only when the
car revs beneath my bum. He glances over his shoulder, tosses
me a wink, and I barely catch the telly as it slips between my
fingertips. *Who was that masked man?*

"—tried to tell you before that the money wasn't in the account for me to pay it last month." I hear Reagan's voice dron-
ing on about my financial strain as I struggle to regain my composure. "Or the month before that—"

"Morning, Ms. Stone," the driver pipes.

"Uh-huh!" I reply in a haze.

"—not after I paid the Saks bill; they were threatening col-
lections. And well, Barney's was—"

I dead the line and bite down ferociously on my freshly manicured nails, gazing into the lavish storefronts of Manhattan's
Upper East Side as we ride down Lexington to the firm with
thoughts of butt nekkid sex and thievery on my mind. But my

thoughts tailspin as I obsess over how I'm going to rob Peter to pay Prada...*and who was that masked man?*

"Yes, Reagan?" I reluctantly answer the cell again as it vibrates, snapping me out of my trance. I'd gotten comfortable dodging bills in the last few months when the economic swine flu had begun to affect the number of new clients I was shuffling through the door.

"Sorry to bother you again, Ms. Stone, but the big bosses have asked to speak with you directly upon your arrival." Her voice is tighter than the tracks Kiki stitched into my head. She whispers emphatically, "It sounds pretty urgent."

3

"Ms. Stone! Wait!" A well-built, chocolatey man yells toward the cab as I struggle to step onto the blurred curb. "Here, let me help you," he offers, reaching down for my hand as I tumble from the cab.

"I, I'm f-fine!" I slightly slur.

"Take my hand, Ms. Stone!" the man with the strong hands orders, reaching out for me. "Take it!"

I center myself and interlock my fingers with his. A shock pulses up my thighs. The three dirty martinis had gone to my head and had apparently ventured off to other body parts as well.

"Looks like you've had a pretty good night."

I smooth down my tailored charcoal skirt and look him in the eye. "It's"—*dunh dunh dunh*—"THE DOORMAN." I sway a smidge and catch my breath, watching his imaginary cape blow in the wind.

"I just got off, but still...let me help you into your building."

"*My* building? Oh, I don't think so," I say, staring up at the fifty-story luxury high-rise. "This won't be *my* building much longer." I look around and point at the old white-haired woman exiting with her handler. "Maybe *her* building, but it won't be MY building!"

"But you've lived here seven years."

"How would you know, you just started here." I fumble through the door and he steadies me in his arms. "You asked about me?" I can't help but notice the bulge in his bicep and the other one quickly hardening in his pants. "Ooh." I tighten my grip around his muscle.

Blushing, he says, "You can't leave me now; we're just getting started."

"Are you flirting with me?" I ask, and swivel my body around to face him.

"I was just saying that—"

"Who are you anyway, Mr. Doorman?"

"Your new concierge, transferred from the Soho property last week," he smiles that same killer-watt smile from this morning. "Apollo." *Epic!*

I look past his hazel eyes over his smooth bald head and into his grown-man stance. *Wow! Magically delicious.* I suck my teeth and purr. "Apollo the Doorman." He blushes and I take that as my cue to slink farther into his personal space. Feeling fiery and fast, I gently press my breasts against his chest. "Well, Apollo the Doorman, I guess you're just going to have to make yourself unforgettable."

"How about I start by seeing you upstairs? Make sure you get in safely." Then he slides the palm of his hand past my ass and rests it in the small of my back, leading me toward the elevator this time. "After all, it's part of my job to make sure nothing happens to you."

I eye him and step into the lift.

"Looks like you've been doing some serious celebrating tonight."

My slick smile turns sour. "I don't know if that's what I'd call it, unless you can celebrate the end of the big dream, the end of the big career, the end—"

"What?"

"I got fired today!" I roll my eyes and fold my arms across my chest.

"Ms. Stone...I'm sorry to hear—"

"Dream killers!"

"Oh, no, you've got it all wrong! I give life back...I don't take it away."

4

The air is warm in the elevator as the doors begin to close. I press for the penthouse.

"I gave them the best seven years of my life, sacrificed everything, and when it's finally my turn, they push me out the door for a blond boy named Biff," I growl into the cramped space. "Said they couldn't make me an offer. 'Our time together has come to an end.' Just like that!" I punch at the steel elevator wall. "Owww!"

Apollo grabs my fist and immediately begins soothing my hand until I calm somewhere between the twentieth and twenty-second floors. "I'm sure you'll find something else."

"There *is* nothing else." I exhale. "That's all I know...all I can do..." My voice dives into a hush. "Practicing law is all I've ever been good at."

"I find that hard to believe," he says, glancing over his shoulder at my long legs. His eyes take me in slowly, moving up my thighs and settling on my breasts. He tilts his head slightly and licks his lips.

The sight of his tongue distracts me, shooting another hot flash up my thighs. I chase it. "You like what you see, Mr. Doorman?" My words are slippery, my thoughts push past racy.

The corners of his seductive mouth turn up. The doors open and he steps aside. "This is where we get off."

"Yes," I ooze back, unsure of where the intense urge to pounce on him is headed, "it sure is, isn't it!"

Apollo's commanding hand brushes against my ass this time as he leads me. The wallpapered hall spins in slow motion, and his grasp steadies me as I slink down the carpet. Swiveling my body around to face him, I lean against my front door and rasp coyly, "Well, aren't you the gentleman...walking me all the way home."

"It's my job to make sure all my tenants are very well taken care of."

"Is that right?" I arch into him, suddenly aware that I haven't had a dick date that didn't require batteries in many moons.

"Yes," he says, without hesitation. "That's right, Ms. Stone."

"And just how much effort do you put into making sure they're satisfied?"

"Well, like you, I'm very good at what I do."

"How good...exactly?" I ask, totally channeling my inner Eartha.

His voice is deliberate, his tone confident. "I've never entertained a complaint."

"And I bet you've serviced your fair share of women in your line of work."

A slick smile appears. "I take my job very seriously."

Maybe it's the dirty martinis or just the dirty little girl who's been locked in her room far too long without any sexual healing, but somewhere in this soft porn flick, I decide to just go for it! I reach out for him and run the back of my hand against his finely sculpted face, down the side of his neck and across his nipples, both now erect. My heart is pounding when I whisper my name: "Phoenix."

"Excuse me?"

I clear my throat and say it with assurance this time. "Phoenix Stone."

He exhales, inches from my neckline. "Such power behind a name like that."

I turn to the door, fumbling with the keys. The effects of the dirty martinis were making a departure, but a dick date with the doorman would be the purrrfect after-party. *Go for it, Penny, you'll never see him after you move out anyway,* the horny red devil on my right shoulder coaxes. *This is hot dick on a stick!* I fight the uncooperative lock that much harder.

"I can help you with that, you know," Apollo offers, leaning down to take the keys from me with ease. His lips brush against my neck as he whispers into my ear, "All you have to do is let go."

Without resisting, I release the keys into his hand. I close my eyes and listen as he successfully unlocks the door. My knees wobble.

"Very good," he approves, seductively. "I can take it from here."

5

The front door swings open and Apollo catches me in his arms before I can fall any farther. *God, I miss the touch of a man.* His arms feel like a lifesaving cure wrapped around my seven-year illness. *Why have I punished Penny so long? Bad Mommy!*

"Thank you for seeing me up to my apartment. I appreciate all the VIP treatment; I'm sure I'll miss that when I'm gone." I drop the Birkin bag to the floor and fight the urge to yank my blouse open. "Who knew the amenities here were so indulgent?" I throw my arms around his neck. *What am I doing?* A hint of leftover cologne has settled into the fibers of his white cotton shirt and its intensity is now more intoxicating than Belvedere. My eyes are heavy as I breathe him in. Slowly, he pulls away. I cling to him and boldly say, "Why, uh—why don't you show me some of the...*amenities* while you're here?"

"I don't think that's part of the agreement." He struggles to release himself from the semi–choke hold.

"Agreement?"

He chuckles, coolly, as he frees himself. "Your lease, Ms. Stone."

"It's Phoenix. Remember?" *And why is he trying to forfeit our game now, a game I'd just joined after nearly a decade of sitting on the sidelines?* I steal his hands and press them against my taut ass, pulling his shirt from his pants and awkwardly running my fingernails over his hard defined abs and up to his nipples. I squeeze them gently and let out a moan the instant I feel my pussy purr. He closes his eyes. His hard-on warrants a deep breath. *Must. Fuck. Him. Now!*

"Now that you're safe and sound, Ms. Stone," he recovers, "I think I'll see myself out."

Say what now?! My inner beast had been released and she wants to roll around in the hay! "Isn't it in your job description to service my needs?" Pouting, I undo the top button on my silky blue blouse.

"Slow down with that." He unravels himself from me again but this time he turns toward the front door. "You've had a lot to drink and your day has you feelin' a little vulnerable right now." He glances at his watch. "This is where I say good night, Ms. Stone." Stopping in his steps to leave me hot and a lot past horny, he says matter-of-factly, "But I really do hope tomorrow works out better for you."

Yeah... NO! This isn't at all how I saw this playing out in my mind. "Apollo!" Frustrated and admittedly stalker-*ish*, I stomp my stiletto into the hardwood.

He doesn't blink. "You're not ready." Without acknowledging my quick dissent into bitch, he turns the doorknob. "And Ms. Stone, you can't just order me to fuck you! That's not at all how this works."

Leaning against the bookcase in the foyer, I feel myself begin to unravel. The only reminder of my tragic evening spent getting dirty with Belvedere is the pounding sound between my ears. "Okay. So just tell me; what *exactly* do I have to do to get ready?" I reach around to unzip my skirt. "Really, just tell me, 'cuz I'm a bit of an overachiever and it doesn't take me long to get ready." I tug at the skirt and drop it like it's hot. "I mean, I'm superspeedy and I can turn this all around in no time flat, just tell me what, how, who...what, *how*—"

"Look, I'm sorry you had such a fucked-up day, really I am, but this isn't what you need to make it better."

Ohhh, I beg to differ, Mr. Doorman! "Uhm, I'm a li'l bit confused," I admit, looking down at my underwear. "So what exactly is it you think I need now?"

"Coffee...maybe a cup of herbal tea."

When did this turn into an episode of "Little Penthouse on the Prairie?" I mumble under my breath, "Um, tea isn't exactly the direction I thought we were headed." *No, sirrr!*

"Excuse me for being so forward, Ms. Stone, but you don't strike me as the kind of woman who invites a stranger up to her apartment for a fuck session." He points at my polka dot panties. "Unless I'm reading this all wrong."

My eyes dart to the floor. *Okay.* On cue, I quickly pull my skirt back up and zip it.

"I'm just being honest. I don't want you to do something

you'll regret tomorrow and I just started here and wouldn't want to..." *Blah blah blah...*

Jaguar sashays into the kitchen, licking her lips and wagging her tail. I swear I hear her meow me a disapproving "loser."

"And you're still not ready."

I tuck my blouse back into my skirt. "Okay, yes, I had a really bad day!" I look up at him and then quickly turn away. "Okay, so it was a really, uh, f'ed-up day. And because of it, I don't know what's gonna happen to me or where I'm gonna live or work or—" I fluster, before shaking myself out of the downward spiral, "but I'm a big girl, ya know and—"

"No, Phoenix, you're one-hundred-percent *woman*."

I smooth down the frizzy damp hair that's come undone around my temple and hold my head high.

"But you're just not ready for what I have to offer."

Deciding to salvage what dignity I have left, I rethink raping him. "You're right; I'm going to be just fine. I may not have any savings, or any investments, or any real assets," I look down at my fifteen-hundred-dollar shoes, "but I'm a big girl, er, uh, woman," I say, pushing my shoulders back, fighting off tears, "and I'm going to be just, just...well, as soon as I figure out how I'm going to pay this damn rent I'm going to be just fine!" I side-eye the shoes again. *Absolutely not!* I fasten the top button of my blouse and turn toward the door to escort Apollo out, swearing my inner crybaby off. "Yep, Penny and I are going to be just fi—"

"So tell me the truth, Phoenix," Apollo steps in front of me and squares my shoulders. He studies me while he runs his fingers over his goatee. Maybe it was the pathetic rant about me being broke, or maybe it was because my in-your-face, fuck-me-now approach had just been totally rejected, but I am suddenly feeling majorly exposed. "When was the last time you felt the touch of a man?"

"I don't really know how to answer that, I mean, well, I guess it's been a while and—"

He traces his fingers over my lips and I shut up.

"...the last time you let someone see you?"

"No one has ever really—"

His finger is still pressed against my lips. "...shown you how it feels to be wanted—"

"Uh, well—"

"...and needed?" His hands grasp the back of my neck. "When was the last time a man made you cum so hard you thought you were going to explode?"

I clutch my pearls and on autopilot, I reach for the top button of my blouse again, this time I unbutton it before he can change his mind. "And who would—"

"Phoenix," he whispers into my ear as he closes the distance between us. He takes my hand and slides it under his shirt and over his throbbing heart. "It's nice to finally meet you."

6

Apollo reaches for my chin and tilts my head straight into his bold eyes. He watches me so long I start to feel naked. *Is he going to kiss me?* No one has really seen me in years. *I think he's going to kiss me.* My thoughts jumble as he leans forward. *I haven't been kissed in nearly two years, three months, one week*—but he passes my mouth only to brush the blade of my shoulder with his lips. I lace my fingers behind his head. He kisses my shoulder again. This time I tense.

"Let go," I hear him say into my skin. "You're a big girl, remember? This is what you said you wanted." I close my eyes, tingling at the touch of his mouth that stops only to bite into my hot skin and torch the rest of me. "Now, let me handle you the right way." On impulse, my back curves into him. "And I want to see you take it like a woman!" *OMG!* I feel myself tense again until he grabs the back of my neck and pulls me into him. "I got this."

The next thing I know I'm in his arms being carried to the living room. *Wow!* He sits me on the sofa and his tongue doesn't miss a beat, licking around my earlobe forcing the thin hairs on my neck to pay attention. My breasts throb through my blouse. They are begging to be next in line. The air is thick. I moan into it, my legs dying to open for him. I wait impatiently as Apollo undresses me with his eyes, showing me every place he intends to spend time. He seems to be in no rush, breathing me in until his eyes finally stop at mine. He kisses me. I freeze.

"Relax."

"But—"

"I told you, baby, I got this!"

"But—" *Man up, Penny!*

He kisses me softly at first, then much harder. *It's game time!* He pulls away slightly and licks my upper lip, tracing over it with his tongue. I'm wet where it matters. *Score!* He sucks on my bottom lip and I inhale his air before he kisses me again, parting my lips with his tongue, slow-dancing in my mouth to the beat of seduction. His eyes are closed, while mine roll back in my head as he makes love to me, has sex with me, and fucks me under the influence of this one brutal kiss. *OMFG!* I am beyond drunk from this man, willingly following his lead, farther away from my comfort zone. When we come up for air, his words cause panic in my ears, "We're taking it all off tonight. I want to see you, every part of you. No mask in sight."

I lean back, unable to completely let go. *Pull up your big girl panties, Penny! We're going in!*

"Isn't this what you said you wanted?"

I nod my head up and down.

"Then play by my rules tonight."

My head bobs up and down again.

"Now, open your legs." It was the last thing I heard him say before he slid his hand between my thighs and massaged his way into my swollen pussy. My insides bubble and an electric surge shoots through me. I gasp for air when he slides a third finger into me to join the other two. Apollo was bringing my sleeping pussy back to life.

"You're tight," he exhales into my lips.

"Uh-huh."

"When was the last time someone fucked you real good?"

Besides Cash?

"And made you cum so hard you squirted?"

I'd heard stories about that but always thought it was an urban myth.

Apollo kneels in front of me and slips his other arm behind me, pulling me onto the edge of the cushion. Rhythmically, he moves his fingers inside me like he's been there before, like he knows his way around, finger-fucking me into delirium. I haven't been finger-fucked since the tenth grade! And I don't remember it feeling anything like this. He props my right leg over his shoulder and the other obediently follows. And with every finger-thrust, each one more powerful that the last, he rocks me deeper into oblivion. When I glance down I see his dick through his denim standing at attention. I lick my lips and feel a sudden urge to get to know him. But before I can make any power moves, he pushes me back onto the couch, shutting me down, putting me back in my place. "My rules," he says, as his free hand travels around my belly and up my torso, stopping just short of my second blouse button. There is instruction in his eyes. I know exactly what he wants me to do. Apollo rubs my left breast over the silky top and I can't unhook my bra fast enough. He takes turns caressing my breasts. We are both in a hot rhythm, moving in sync with each other's beats. He squeezes my nipple between his fingers and I'm certain I'm going to...erupt. Right then. Explode. *Right there.*

"Right there!" I swear, groaning into the air, now scented with sex. Like a magician, he continues to fuck me with three fingers, my G-spot now under his spell, and erotically massages my breasts while exploring my mouth with his tongue.

"Oh, god!" I hear myself testify. My legs are in the air, hovering over his head somewhere, my hands wrapped around the back of his neck. "Oh, god!"

He orders, "Let go and cum for me!"

"OH, GOD!" The orgasmic ride snakes down my spine and slithers straight through me. "OHHH, GODDD..."

7

Who is this masked man? My body spasms through the aftermath of small orgasms. Nerve endings are tingly and my eyes are still rolling around in my head. Apollo slides his soaked fingers from inside me and licks each of them. "You taste as good as I knew you would." His penetrating voice makes me want to hop on all fours and bow down. I feel his other hand unbuttoning the last two buttons on my blouse and I wriggle free from it. The soft silk is like a razor against my skin as it slides down my arms. I purr as he leaves a trail of kisses past my neck straight into my breasts. I sit up to watch when he stops to give them his full attention. The sharp smell of cum has settled into the air. I breathe it in, flinching when he squeezes my breasts. *That hurts so good.* He bites down on his lips and within seconds, my nipples are between his teeth. I pull away from the painful pleasure.

"Take it," he orders.

I gasp into submission and watch him caress my breasts, then lick them, suck them and devour them all over again. Without instruction this time, my fingers find my swelling clit.

I am totally spellbound. Watching his head buried between my breasts I hear, "Now, I want your pussy. Put it in my mouth." *Oh, Penny!* Apollo is on his knees, pressing my thighs farther apart. He smoothes his hand across my bare pussy and in one beat, two of his fingers slither inside me while his tongue bathes my clit. The room turns every shade of purple and I swear a white glow encircles him. "Oh, god!" I am moaning so loud. *The neighbors!* He stops to glide his tongue over my liquid lips, coveting each of them. When I feel like I'm going to crawl straight out of my skin, I grab the back of his head. My back bends into a perfect arch as he starts to tongue-fuck me. My French tips dig deeper into him. My wet thighs throttle him. My legs are wrapped around his head and I am somewhere deep in his mouth. I feel my body rising from the couch and realize Apollo has picked me up and is headed toward the bedroom— with me in midair and my pussy mid tongue-fuck. He doesn't miss a beat or a thrust, or a lick or a suck as he carries me down the foyer, around the corner, into the kitchen, past the dressing room...straight through the pearly gates.

8

Apollo unzips my skirt and tosses it to the floor in my bedroom. He moves like a master and I watch every move he makes. I can't pull my eyes away from him. *Epic.* He stands over me, running his hands over my thighs and down my legs. *This must be what the champagne room in heaven feels like.*

"I want to know what you feel like." My stomach knots. "But I need to see what you look like first." *See?*

Before he can reach for the light switch, I grab his arm.

"Wait, I don't think—"

"Wait?" he chuckles, grabbing the back of my hair. "This is my game, darlin'; do as you're told."

Okay. My fingers go limp and I release his arm and surrender.

He flips the light switch. It flickers before spotlighting me.

"Now, stand up." As I lower my body to the floor, he says, "Not on the floor...the bed."

I balance myself on the plush duvet.

He moves toward me. "Turn around." He licks his lips, tilting his head to the side. "Slowly."

I obey.

He runs his hand over his smooth head and across the back of his neck before unbuckling his leather belt. A part of me wants to know what comes next. The other part wants him to bend me over and spank me. Our eyes lock as his denim rattles against the hardwood. His boxer-briefs fit snugly around his bulging dick and I am dying to feel it between my jaws, shoved down my throat. He unbuttons his shirt, never taking his eyes from my thighs.

"I can see you."

I fidget with my hands behind my back. "And?"

"I like it."

My face burns red as I blush.

"Come take these off," he nods down at his briefs. "Get on your knees," he commands, eyeing the floor. Without blinking, I drop to all fours and slink toward him. My index fingers grip the elastic waistband, and as I pull them down, his hard ribbed dick rises to greet my mouth. *Well, hello!* He wraps my hair around his hand and yanks my head back, my mouth now wide open, and thrusts his dick between my cheeks. I suck my new BFF slowly at first, then faster and harder, stopping only when he grabs the back of my neck and pulls me in. My pussy sizzles when I feel the tip of his dick slide deeper down my throat. I massage his balls, tickling around them until he finally frees me from his grip. I wrap my mouth around each of them, devouring them to the sound of improvised hums and impromptu moans. *What would Jenna do?* I line my grip with spit and with his dick between both hands, I rotate my stroke in opposing motion. I give him head until my mouth is numb. The throbbing pulse in his dick tells me he wants to cum, but before he does he yanks my head back by my hair and yells into the air, "FUCKKK!"

9

"It's time for me to fuck you."

I hesitate. Everything around me is moving in slow motion.

"Now!"

His words sting down my spine as he throws me onto the bed and straddles me. Apollo dips his fingers into my pussy to test the temperature, puts them in his mouth. "You taste so good." He rubs my liquid lips with the tip of his dick. I grip the satin sheet beneath me and remind myself to breathe. "Let go. I got you, baby."

"Yes," I hear myself murmur. Inch by unbelievable inch my pussy stretches out to take him.

"I want to hear you!"

He is over me, his chest shiny with sweat, glazing his super-human body. "Yes!"

"Louder!" He orders into my ear.

"OH, MY GOD!"

He kisses me; his tongue is slick, his thrusts harder. The ride speeds toward wild. His motion is ripped with power. The electric black air is pulsing around me. I let go and wrap my legs around his waist. He throws them over his shoulders instead, and fucks me with savage intensity. My back bends when he slips his arm behind it and flips me over to straddle him. I carve my nails into his abs, my pussy now swallowing him.

"That's right; take all of it!" he commands, and palms my cheeks, digging deeper into me. I throw my head back and gasp. He slaps my ass, branding a welt into my skin. I can feel him everywhere. My pussy tightens around him, stroking him up and down, sucking him in as the ride rocks from side to side. He slaps me again, my skin stinging. "Very good," he says, tasting my breasts. As I master the rhythm and soul of his flow, my toes curl.

"Come up here and sit on my face," he orders. I slip in and out of ecstasy as I climb him. He tastes me first, then begins to own me, forcing my face into the headboard. My pelvis snakes around his mouth as his tongue teases my clit. His fingers trail the dripping sweat down the curve of my back, straight into my asscrack. I shriek into the damp air as he slips in a second finger to fuck me dirty. His tongue is wrapped around my clit as I grind my hips between his lips. My head spins as the ride picks up speed.

I can't breathe. I gasp for air. As I'm exhaling, he swings my thigh over his head and tosses me roughly around the wet bed. My screams, now muffled in the duvet, hit a feverish pitch as he fucks me from behind. His breathing is heavy, his moans now louder each time he rams his dick deeper into me. He wraps his fingers around my throat causing my clit to almost explode. Cream covers my fingers as I tour my pussy toward climax. He chokes me, fucking me wildly, until I feel a hot stream of cum shoot from inside of me—"OH, GOD!"—squirting all over me.

I look down in raw confusion and he orders me to "Let it flow!"

I cry out in unimaginable ecstasy, "Oh, GAWD!"

Barely able, I roll over and palm his rock-hard dick, deep-throating it until it's beating stronger than my heart. He grabs my head and pulls me into him until his body shocks.

"Open your mouth!"

I obey and his milky cum explodes all over my face.

10

Sooo totally better than Turks & Caicos! I replay the highlights of our fuck session in my mind as I finish washing Apollo off me. Jaguar prances into the bathroom and licks her lips. *I know, right!* Smothered in afterglow, I tie the silk robe around my waist and spy Apollo-the-Fucking-God leaning against the front door. *Amen.*

"I can see you now," he repeats.

I clear my throat. "Yes. And..."

"I like what I see."

I glance at the floor.

"Look at me."

My eyes travel up his body, straight into his eyes. "Did you like being fucked like that?"

I feel a chill and nod.

He smiles that familiar killer smile.

"Is there more?" I ask, in a hushed voice.

"Maybe you *are* a big girl. You think you can handle more?"

I nod again, anxious to get on the waiting list.

"There may be something we can do about that." He unloosens my robe in a swift move and studies the curves of my body. "And both get what we want."

He reaches into his pocket and pulls out a thick wad of money. As he counts off several big bills, he orders me to take a shower and rest up. "But first, this is for you."

"What?" I shake my head in confusion. "What's this?"

"Take it."

"But...but...I can't take—"

"Yeah, you can." He wraps my fingers around the cash. "You earned it."

I step back. "You're paying me! For, for, *SEX!*"

"You were worth it."

OM-fucking-G!

"But, I'm not...I'm not..." I whisper, "*a hooker!*"

"No, you're not. You're more like a *girlfriend* experience."

I gasp and clutch my pearls.

"You need to recognize your worth, Ms. Stone, and put a price on that pussy; it should be your most valuable asset."

Pussy PROPERTY? "Look, Apollo, I never expected to get paid for—"

"I know you didn't. But now that you have, you need to rethink your pricing strategy. You're in business for yourself now—if I remember correctly. And you said you wanted to make partner, *partner*." He chuckles, and I begin to think this is all a joke until he reaches for the door and says, "It's worth a lot more than that, by the way. I just took my cut." He glances at the cash I'm now gripping tightly in my hand. "My clients will pay whatever you ask." He nods toward the corridor. "And they're in the building; you'll never need an umbrella. Just keep the polka dots."

"But, but, you're the doorman?"

"Yeah, and?" he challenges. "What exactly do you think my job is all about?"

I furrow my brow, seeing *him* for the first time tonight.

"You were the one who said my job is to provide a service, right? Well, how is this any different?"

I slowly close my robe and double-knot it as I process what

he's saying. "So you would be, like, my pim—"

"Agent." On cue, that slick smile resurfaces. "Think about it and get back to me. Just don't take too long; people with long paper get impatient. They have options." He reaches out and touches my chin. "But now I can say with certainty that none are as satisfying as you."

He TEST-drove me!

The cash is heavy in my hands. *And he liked the ride!* I steady myself against the wall. My eyes are burning. My mouth is dry. My pussy is hot. Hypnotized, I grip the cash in my hands and the tips of my fingers begin to tremble. *An escort?* I begin to count...my heart pounds as I approach one thousand, my legs weaken as I fly past two thousand. Could I? The familiar scent of the money intoxicates me all over again. My pussy rages as I hit three thousand....

"Fuck! Five thousand doll—*twice a week. Ten thousand. Forty Gs a month. Four hundred and eighty grand a year!* I quickly did the math, willfully blocking out the way I'd be making rent.

Girlfriend experience. Apollo's description runs through my head. Funny how a little game of semantics could put a different face on things. I glance down at Penny. *Could I fuck my way out of my financial woes?* She purrs. *Should I?* I close my eyes and smell the cash. *Would I?*

I look up at Apollo. But he is gone.

THE SANGRIA SEDUCTION

Teddy Bell

I love hearing the "F" word.

—Teddy Bell

"This beautiful woman needs something sweet and tasty, just like her," I tell the attractive and smiling waitress at Chevy's Restaurant. "Two lemon sangrias, please." I don't always order for my dates but my gut feeling is that Lissa Lawton is the type of chick who appreciates a man taking control.

"I hope you don't mind. I think you'll love it." Judging by the faint smile on her lips, I can tell that she didn't.

"It's okay. I trust you, Chris."

Trust. What a beautiful word. This is going easier than I anticipated. "So tell me about yourself, but not the Lissa from eight to five. I want to know the *after*-hours Lissa."

Whatever she is going to tell me, I already know. Lissa Lawton, thirty-two years old, born and raised in Walnut Creek, California, graduated Magna Cum Laude from UC Berkeley with a degree in finance, and then went on to receive her MBA from the Wharton School in Pennsylvania. She's worked in executive management at IBM, Charles Schwab, and Microsoft. She was featured in *Black Enterprise Magazine* as one of the top five future leaders to watch. It's amazing what you can learn on Facebook, LinkedIn and Google.

Today, Lissa is Senior Vice President of Consumer Finance for Wells Fargo Bank in San Francisco. She's single with beautiful golden brown skin and light brown eyes. To me, she bears a striking resemblance to Alicia Keys, the R&B songstress, except that her hair is always pulled up in a tight bun or ponytail. She also wears rimless, oval-shaped, prescription eyeglasses that keep her attractiveness on the down low. Her professional and ultraconservative style smacks of Lily Librarian, but my experienced eyes know that underneath that boring business attire hides a naughty girl with a very gorgeous body. I know her type—quiet, meticulous, dedicated, overworked and socially introverted. My educated guess is that she's probably had one or two relationships that didn't last long because work always came first. Bottom line: the playah in me says she is the perfect candidate to turn up, around and *out*. The only question in my mind is, how long will it take for me to turn nice into nymph?

Okay, before you get your neck all wound up and throw your finger in my face to call me all kinds of bastards, dogs, and man whores, hear me out. I'm not unlike every other man out there who likes a challenge, and I'm not out to hurt anybody. In fact, I'm just the opposite. I, Mr. Christopher Thomas, can be quite the sweetheart. Some may think I'm a thirty-three-year-old playah, but I'd like to think of myself as Mr. Opportunity. True, I brought two Senior Ball dates to the Skyline High School Prom in Oakland; had a hot affair with a Latina counselor at

Laney Community College; and had a sexy San Jose State math professor want to divorce and leave her weak-ass husband for me. I had to shut that down quick because I'm not into long-term commitments just yet.

I'm the kind of man that guys praise and idolize while women either can't get enough of me or hate me because they can't have me. Maybe it's my six-foot-three lean but chiseled physique or possibly my smooth, mocha brown skin tone. And ever since I've been rolling with this nicely trimmed goatee, I have been mistaken for Hollywood actor Idris Elba, a comparison that certainly doesn't hurt my game.

I'm educated, successful and easy on the eyes. When given the opportunity, I know how to make women *feel good* because I'm in tune with their emotions and can read them like a poker player's face. Consider me as a rescue team of sorts...resuscitating poor, pent-up and inhibited damsels in sexual distress and turning them out. Trust me, there are a lot of happy brothas out there that need to be thanking me.

Okay, now that we've got that straight, back to my date with Lissa. I'd just asked her what she did in her spare time.

"Well, I don't have a lot of free time, but when I do I like to read novels or good poetry. Mostly I just veg out on CNN."

"You like poetry?" I ask, about to get my sensitive, cultured man on.

"Some."

"I *love* poetry. I find sonnets very provocative and...well, sexy. Langston, Maya, Sonya Sanchez, Nikki G and Saul Williams are my favorites. In fact, poetry is kinda a hobby of mine," I inform her while looking directly into her light browns.

"Do you write any?" she asks, right on cue. I take the opportunity to put my *I'm thinking* face on as I search the chapbook in my head for an appropriate stanza to throw on her.

"*I plant my two lips into your garden of passion with hopes your sunshine eyes will bloom a bouquet of eternal kisses.*"

"Omigod. That's beautiful. Did you just make that up?" Lissa says. The awe is written all over her face.

"You're quite the muse."

"That was about me?"

"Yeah, it is," I tell her, throwing a little *aw shucks* look on my face.

"Really? Chris, stop messing with me."

"I'm serious. I hope you like it," I say while gently caressing her hand.

"But you don't even know me," she replies while adjusting her glasses and blushing.

Oh, but I do, I think while giving her a half smile.

Lissa may think it's a coincidence that we met at the Wells Fargo Bank building in San Francisco two weeks ago, but it was anything but. The first time I saw her was about a month ago at the downtown Oakland 24 Hour Fitness club. She was jogging on a treadmill and didn't notice me shooting hoops, but I sure did notice her. She was wearing one of those purple spandex body suits and a long blue T-shirt. She was trying to be modest and cover up, but she must have gotten hot because she pulled the T-shirt off to mop her sweaty face and almost blew my head off in the process. She was about five feet six, 130 pounds with a perky set of happy-to-see-you 36Cs. Her stomach was Beyoncé flat with a waistline an hourglass would envy. The guy jogging next to her looked over and made some kind of comment she obviously didn't appreciate because she rolled her eyes and immediately hopped off the treadmill and split. That's when I discovered two things about her: one, her body is slammin', and two, for me to have a chance at tappin' that I would have to approach her nice and easy. Most times I just go for it, but instinct told me to be patient with this one.

I found out Lissa's name from one of the fitness instructors and then, with the help of Facebook and LinkedIn, learned that her office was just three blocks away from mine in San Francisco. The next day, I came to work early and hung around the Wells Fargo building in order to conveniently run into her. Three times that week, we *bumped* into each other and shared a bit of casual conversation. When it became clear that Lissa was feeling more comfortable with me, I suggested we meet for drinks. I recommended the following Tuesday, just so she wouldn't think it was a date. She paused before saying yes, but I could tell she was game. No doubt she's one of those "nothing is a coincidence" kind of sisters. To make her feel even more in control, I didn't ask for her number or anything, just told her to meet me at Chevy's—a perfect meet-a-colleague-after-work kind of spot. No pressure.

For the rest of the week, I couldn't stop imagining how exciting it would be to bring out the freak in her. It's like clipping a virgin's wings, knowing you're the one she will always remember. I kept picturing her standing there looking so pure and innocent, totally unaware that she was the chosen prey. Usually I date attractive women who have no money or rich women who don't know how to please a man. Very rarely do I find a sexy woman who is rich *and* pleases me sexually, but there's something about this educated, overworked, professional and sexually repressed woman that tells me this chick might be the one.

So now, after waiting five days, here we are at Chevy's.

"Here are your lemon sangrias," announces the waitress, winking at me with her seven digits on my napkin. I ignore her. I'm on a mission.

"Lissa, I have a problem."

"Okay..." she says, not quite sure what to think.

"My problem is that I don't know you as well as I'd like to. We should change that. Spend more time together..."

"I don't really date much." she says nervously. "I mean, with work and everything. There's just no time."

"You know what they say, all work and no play makes Lissa..."

"Yeah, yeah, a dull girl. I know, but I can't help it. Work I'm good at. But dating is a whole different thing."

"You're just out of practice, because I can't imagine why a girl as fine as you..." I stop myself, knowing that between the poetry and the gentle compliments, she's definitely getting ripe for the pickin'. No need to push too hard. "Promise me something."

"Maybe."

I take that as a full-out yes. "Promise me that you will have three dates with me."

"Three dates?"

"Yes, three. And if you don't have a wonderful time on each one, I'll never bother you again."

"Well...I...I don't know.... I'm in the middle of this project and I know I have to go to Pasadena for a conference in a few weeks...and maybe Spain, and...well..."

"And what?"

"And, uh, well I'm kind of already interested in someone."

I'm not buying that tired line for a nanosecond. All the time I spent scoping her out not once did I see, hear or infer any interest in or by any man other than her fuddy-duddy boss, old man Alexander—and believe me, even to eyes way less experienced than mine, that is all about business.

"Just three," I say smiling but with sternness. "Come on, live a little. Besides, I'm in a real writing groove and you're my muse. You can't leave me hangin'. Trust me, you'll have a good time. I promise."

Lissa smiles and sighs. I know it is a done deal.

"All right, three dates," she says. "Chris, don't take this the wrong way but I'm not looking to start any kind of intimate or romantic relationship...okay?"

"I'm cool with that. I'm just looking to make a new friend and write a little poetry." I raise my glass. "To new and exciting friendships."

She raises hers and taps my glass before taking a sip. My eyes peer over the top of mine, taking her in with the sangria.

"Mmm...this is really good!"

Baby, I want to say to her, you don't know the half of it.

It's been a week since I met with Lissa at Chevy's. As luck would have it, Costco, the company I work for as an operations consultant, decided to do business with Wells Fargo and assigned me to the task. My girl has no idea that we are going to be playing *and* working together. But let's not jump ahead. Right now, I'm working on making her feel relaxed and getting her to open up a little on our first date.

We're at Serendipity's Hair Salon in Oakland. The moment Lissa enters the salon, my eyes immediately recognize those curves from the gym. She's wearing some bootylicious Dereon jeans and a blue and gold UC Berkeley sweatshirt with blue gladiator sandals. Her simple weekend outfit is far hotter than her weekday Wells Fargo business suits. Okay, two points for the little lady.

My cousin Peaches loaned me her shop for a couple of hours. For our first date I've planned a Sunday afternoon pampering session. She is reluctant at first; I guess seeing the shop lit up with scented candles, with smooth jazz music and homemade lemon sangrias set off her "this looks like a date" alarm. But she quickly becomes receptive when she sees Peaches, just as I'd planned, here to help break the ice.

"Just relax and let Peaches take care of you. Clear your mind. The only thing you should be thinking about is being free," I softly whisper in Lissa's ear while my cousin slowly massages a rosemary and peppermint hair conditioner into her scalp. Her head is lying back in a sink while her body is comfortably re-clined in Peaches' salon chair.

"...Free from work, free from stress, free from everything."

"Mmm..." Lissa murmurs. I smile. That's the sensual sound I love my women to make!

"Shh. Close your eyes." She happily obeys. "I want you to imagine a summer breeze blowing through your hair, releasing all negative thoughts and lingering tension," I command softly as I pull my cell phone from my pocket.

The peaceful atmosphere is broken up by my phone call-ing the salon. "Cuz, can you take over while I get the phone?" Peaches asks with a wink in her voice. She's not the best ac-tress in the world, but at least she's down with helping a brother out. As per our plan, Peaches won't be coming back, leaving me alone with my beautiful freak in the making.

"Lissa, you don't mind?" I ask, knowing she's already too far gone to resist.

"Mmm..." is all she can manage.

My hands start at the back of her neck and slowly work up to the top of her scalp. My finger massage technique is working its magic. Lissa's eyes remain closed and I can tell her mind is completely open to my touch. I can measure her pleasure quo-tient just by the way she is breathing. "...And now I want you to imagine warm rain washing your long beautiful hair."

Damn! I'd underestimated how striking Lissa's face is. It is so soft and angelic. Lissa never wears noticeable makeup but I am imagining her kissable full lips coated in red lipstick. My lustful eyes can't stop caressing her entire body and I have to admit that the sight and my accompanying thoughts are making my big magic stick stiff. As sexy as I thought she was, she's even sexier right in front of me.

With my right hand I begin rinsing the conditioner out of her hair with warm water while my free left hand continues massaging suds out of her scalp. The more I pamper Lissa, the more I am really getting into what I am doing. The excitement of her beauty has streams of blood rushing to my willy, but I have to remain cool and calm.

"That was wonderful, Chris. Thank you," Lissa gushes as I sit her up and towel dry her hair.

"I'm not done yet. There's more. Well, there was but Peaches had an emergency. So if you don't mind me finishing up…"

"More? That hair washing was amazing. As they say, you got skills," she says, already beginning to twist her hair back into a knot.

"Your hair is so beautiful. Why don't you ever wear it down?"

"I don't know. It's just easier to keep it up and out of my way. I don't like fussing with my appearance."

"Well, reconsider. You're already gorgeous but when it's down, even wet you look prettier and more radiant. Don't think I'm BSing you, but Alicia Keys could be your sister."

She blushes with gratification as I move her salon chair straight and upright and give her a glass of lemon sangria, then grab a stool and place it right next to her feet. I remove Lissa's sandals before rubbing some jasmine-scented massage oil on my hands. I can tell by her bright eyes that she is getting excited. That and the fact that she's let her hair back down.

"Close your eyes," I command.

As soon as Lissa closes her eyes, I move my stool closer and elevate her feet to my lap. I begin rubbing the heels of her size-sevens with oiled hands. Her feet are well cared for but are dying for the affection that I am more than willing to give. I gradually massage upward to the middle of her arches in small circular motions. After several minutes her lips part and I can hear small but potent sighs of pleasure leaving her mouth. Lissa's drink is slowly tipping over as her hands become as relaxed as the rest of her body. I take the glass of sangria, pour what is left in my hands and massage it into her feet and toes. Amorously I begin sucking each of her toes, now flavored with lemon sangria. I lick her toes so well that Lissa's satisfied purr is a signal to push farther.

Lissa's eyes are closed but she knows exactly what I am doing, and the sheen of pleasure across her face tells me she likes it. I continue sucking each toe on her right foot while I gently place her left foot directly on my growing cock. Every time she tries to move it away, I make sure her foot remains. I want her to *feel* my hardness.

"What...are...you doing?" she asks while trying to catch her breath.

I want to laugh. Sistergirl has apparently caught herself leaving her comfort zone and getting lost in the adventurous waters of rapture. But I don't stop because I am really getting into this sensual foot bath. Plus, while she was initially shocked, she loves what's happening. To make my point, I start at her heel and draw my tongue up the length of her sole, punctuating the act by taking her middle toe in my mouth and sucking it like a nipple on one of her glorious tits. She gasps. I stop long enough to say, "I'm licking my name on the bottom of your feet...so that if you ever get lost, you'll always find your way back to me."

Hearing my poetic flow, Lissa lets out a stronger sigh. She is breathing more rapidly, while her top teeth devour her lower lip. Her pelvis won't sit still. Lissa's legs stiffen slightly as her hands grip the arms of the salon chair, signaling to me that she is on the verge of orgasm. But just before she reaches the point of ecstasy, I abruptly stop. Lissa's eyes slowly open and her face is flushed. She looks around, confused, as if she doesn't know where she is. Before she can say anything, I let go of her feet and say it is time for us to leave.

Three days after our *spa-licious* date, I have a private meeting at the bank with dreary faced Wells Fargo CEO J. Brunson Alexander. My business plan this afternoon is two-fold—one, to secure the coventure between the bank and Costco, and two, to run an innocent little head trip on Lissa, who I haven't seen or spoken to since drinking sangria from between her toes. I know her office is right next to Mr. Dull Guy, and I make damn sure that she sees me leaving. Lissa tries to catch me at the elevator, but fails. By the time I get back to my office, she's called and left messages on my cell phone that I do not return. I know that I'm all up in her head now, confusing her and filling her mind with questions.

See, the thing is, women like Lissa, women who lack confidence in their womanly selves, will always think that they're the ones screwing up. Women like this constantly accept blame. The trick is to feed and nurture that mindset and get her to depend on me to free her.

A day later, I surprise Lissa with an "apology" bouquet of white lilies and an invitation to join me Saturday at Yoshi's Restaurant and Jazz Club in Jack London Square in Oakland. My plan for our second date is to make Lissa feel special by taking her to a VIP listening party for R&B crooner, Maxwell.

Now that her libido is awakening, Lissa needs a bigger hit of my brand of seduction.

I'm sitting in the front right near the stage waiting for Lissa. The concert starts at 10:00 p.m. I'm pretty sure that unless it involves a business report of some kind, Lissa is not a night owl and has never been to this place. But I'm also positive that these two facts will not keep her away. I'll bet my pimp playah card on it. I haven't heard from her but I have no doubt that she will show. I am a temptation too great for her to resist. She's definitely feeling me and I know those head and foot massages have planted subliminal seeds in her mind to be more open and free with me. It's time to massage the middle. The naughty girl in her is beginning to surface. Everything is going perfect as planned. And tonight I plan to help Lissa step into her dark and sexy side.

Lissa arrives just before the show begins and unknowingly has me throwing away the two business cards I received from flirtatious tarts I encountered earlier. She is clearly the most beautiful woman in the club. Her long, silky hair is loose and brushed to the side, covering her left shoulder. I also see the sheen of a bronze-colored lipstick that matches her brown silk blouse and skirt. She wears a thick black belt to accentuate her waist and some three-inch-high, black peep-toe pumps that make her calves flex every time she takes a step. With no pre-scription glasses in sight, her glowing light browns are revealed. Bitch is hot! Amazing what a little bit of the right attention will do for a girl.

The moment Lissa gets near me the band starts playing and Maxwell appears on the stage singing his popular song, "Ascension (Don't Ever Wonder)." Amid the sexy innuendos and outright propositions, the mostly female audience applauds thunderously.

"I'm so glad you came," I stand and tell Lissa in her ear before kissing her on the cheek. With a gentleman's flair, I pull out the chair and help her sit at the table. "I thought you might be mad with me."

"I appreciate a sincere apology and white lilies even more, but we can talk about the other stuff later. For now, let's just enjoy the show," she utters in my ear trying to speak over the loud music.

"I ordered some lemon sangrias. That's our drink right?"

"Yes," she responds with a slight smile.

Bringing her to see Maxwell was no *willy-nilly* move. It is as premeditated, predetermined, pre-I'm-gonna-rock-your world, as they come. Maxwell has mastered the knack of filling the head and the drawers of every female his music touches with fantasies of seductive sex. Tonight he's playing on my team—a warmup act if you will—opening the mind and hopefully the legs of the lovely Lissa.

My boy does not disappoint and is putting on a great show. Song after song he has the females in the crowd excited and screaming for more. After a second round of sangria, Lissa doesn't mind my adventurous back touches or occasional thigh brushes. When she laughs at my jokes she sometimes touches my arm, shoulder or back. I'm reading that as an open invitation to move in closer, which I do. I close the space between our chairs so that my left hand can touch the small of her back. Soon that same hand is traveling to the top of her tempting thigh. The higher my hand moves the more her skin's temperature seems to rise. My eyes never look directly at Lissa, only at the stage. My hand mischievously slides down to her knees, gently parts them, and proceeds to caress her inner thigh. I let my hand rest there while Maxwell sings "Pretty Wings." Lissa nervously sips and toys with her sangria, never looking directly at me, but at this juncture, eagerly anticipating my next move.

While the club crowd focuses on Maxwell's slow but high-pitched *ooohs* and *aaahs* under the dim lights, my fingers travel farther north to find some very moist panties. I press softly against Lissa's warm clit without anyone near us noticing. Lissa's legs open slightly wider under the table as my exploring hand becomes soaked in her juices. I move my fingers in small and rhythmic circles that are in sync with the music. Her waist and hips slightly gyrate to make it easier for my fingers to do their work. Lissa is more than willing to comply. She is under my spell and I have her exactly where I want her. Her mouth withholds the passionate screams her body desperately wants to release. My fingers become more aggressive, assertive and unrelenting. I want her to suffer complete pleasure in silence. Lissa halfheartedly tries brushing my hand away but does not continue to fight when I ignore her. For three straight songs I massage her drenched vagina nonstop, bringing her to several mini-orgasms. She is so turned on that she's now oblivious to the crowd, the band and Maxwell's crooning. Her eyes are closed and she periodically licks her parched lips trying to maintain what little composure is left, but my fingers moves feverishly, knowing she has one full-blown orgasm left in her.

"Cum again, Lissa, cum hard for Daddy!" I whisper smack in her ear.

"Why...are you...doing this to me...?" Lissa murmurs as she tries to hide her words as if she were a ventriloquist.

"Okay, then YOU do it to you," I insist, taking her hand and gently guiding it into her pussy with mine.

"Release yourself, baby, and be free...cum...cum hard for Daddy NOW!" I demand of her while my hand guides her fingers deeper into her twat.

Almost simultaneously, while Maxwell belts out long and

sexy falsetto notes that have the women erupting in applause, Lissa screams along in orgasmic pleasure. No one is the wiser, except for me and my magic fingers.

"Now taste yourself," I dare her. My dick jumps hard against my jeans as my wish becomes her command. I have to touch my cock as she slowly inserts her hand into her mouth, dripping her tasty pussy juice onto her tongue. Oh, yeah, the horny little genie is coming out of her bottle and not a moment too soon.

Her deliciously slutty move, while a distinct turn-on for me, apparently embarrasses her enough to require an immediate trip to the ladies room. Maxwell launches into his encore performance for the already frenzied crowd. When Lissa returns, I am gone.

Once again, I purposely have not called Lissa all week. I knew that I'd see her at the upcoming bank meeting, plus my "tease her, dog her" plan is progressing right on schedule and is about to bear some seriously delicious fruit. I've awakened Lissa's libido, tamed it and now plan on owning it.

I walk into the meeting, not sure what I'll find but not worried. J. Brunson Alexander is out of the office on sick leave, but gave the meeting facilitator role to Lissa for our Wells/Costco Payment Processing venture. She doesn't speak or look at me during the first few minutes of the meeting. She acts very businesslike, as if she doesn't know me. That shit is just turning me on all the more.

And the girl is looking quite stunning. Desire is definitely transforming her. I knew it would but didn't have a clue to what extent. Her lips are now painted a vibrant red; her hair is down and filled with natural curls that flow just past her shoulders. She's sporting a paper white, silk V-neck blouse that provides a peek of her enticing cleavage and goes well with her tight, black pin-striped pencil skirt that hits just below the knees to reveal those smokin' legs of hers. Legs, I must add, which are made even more tempting by some sheer, black stockings with black sling-back, pointed-toe pumps. My eyes are discreet but she definitely has my mind's attention. In fact, it is hard to think of anything else but those tasty legs wrapped around my waist.

The 4:00 p.m. meeting includes ten executive managers seated around a huge round table while several others attend via conference call line. Lissa passes out an agenda sheet to all in attendance, but the document she gives me is quite different:

Let me
feed myself to you
with hands dipped
in my moist honey
please lick my fingers
taste me, kiss me, let me
lick myself off your lips
while you slide your throbbing heat
in between my mountain peaks
I lock you in and
rock you closer
you drip sticky love
onto my tongue
I suck you in deep
to nurse you
and ask if...
you got milk baby?

My jaw drops. The note throws me off and surprises me. I had bested my record. In less than three dates, I'd turned this simple, workaholic, goody-two-shoes girl out and haven't even sealed the deal yet. Sitting here not being able to touch her is pure torture. Watching and imagining what I am going to do to her gives me an erection the size of a Louisville slugger. Several times during the meeting, I have to cover and adjust myself. I can't wait for this stupid gathering to end.

The meeting goes on for about three and half hours. Although Lissa and I both present project plan items, we continue with our game of not acknowledging each other. At the meeting's conclusion, I inform my colleagues that I need extra time to confirm some things with Miss Lawton. Lissa concludes her good-byes to coworkers and starts putting paperwork into a briefcase. It's after 7:30 p.m. and the conference room is now clear.

"So did you like my poem?" Lissa queries from across the room.

"Yeah, you surprised me, it is really hot."

"Well, you're not the only muse in the room."

"I didn't even know you wrote poetry."

"I don't. This was a first. Just like my hair and foot massage, and you fingering me in public." She is saying all of this as she slinks towards me with slide to her glide that is all about S.E.X. She pulls up on me, her tremendous tits just inches away from my pecs. Shit, my dick is thumping like a garden hose with the faucet on full blast.

"Well, do you want another first?" I ask, reclaiming my cool while moving in on her lips.

"I was hoping you already knew the answer to that question," she purrs.

The Wells Fargo Conference Room on the twentieth floor is off the hook, with spectacular panoramic views of downtown San Francisco, the Golden Gate Bridge, the Bay Bridge, and the Berkeley Hills, but none can compete with the sight standing in front of me now. Lissa slowly takes off her glasses and tosses them on the conference table. Looking into those light brown eyes, I see only want and desire. I brush my lips against hers and feel electric heat travel down my spine and tickle my already erect cock. She calmly takes her fingers, travels underneath her skirt and panties, and touches her own wetness before placing her fingers into my thirsty mouth. I lick each finger slowly, savoring the taste. With no words spoken, we decide to have a passionate ménage à trois with the cityscape.

We start unbuttoning and unzipping each other, yearning to satisfy a sexual hunger that intensifies with every second. Our clothes are all over the conference room floor while my hands explore every line and curve of her sexy body. I kiss her neck, shoulders, breasts, waist and perfect apple bottom. I kneel on one knee while my hands stretch high to tickle her erect, chocolate nipples. She drapes her left thigh over my right shoulder and I softly tongue-kiss her wet and neatly shaved kitty kat. This surprises and stops me dead in my tracks.

"You like?" she asks with a coyness in her voice I'd never heard before.

"Yes, baby, I do." I ain't never lied. Lissa is no longer that conservative librarian but my very own *freak-a-narian*, who shaved her pussy just for me. Totally excited, my tongue licks, twirls and flicks directly on her clit, until her little man in the boat capsizes. The rush of intensity causes her to dig her fingernails deep into my shoulders. She shivers and squirts on my lips that are now painted with her warm, sweet juices.

Lissa abandons all inhibition and lets lustful desire consume her. She stands upright. Her hands touch and admire my massive pecs and six-pack abs. She grabs what I think is a glass of water but is actually lemon sangria, and pours it all over my nakedness. Her tongue travels all across my wet body, finding each drop and licking it off. She softly bites my nipples, sending electric charges throughout my body. She moves farther south to kiss my stomach and lick the sun tattoo that surrounds my navel. She grabs my massive manhood, softly stroking and holding it as if it were her pet snake. Lissa takes my love muscle and slips it in between her C-cups. She uses her hands to make her breasts jiggle and massage me. She slightly tucks her neck so that her mouth can suck on the tip of my penis, making it grow longer. My hands caress the beautiful long hair that I've washed and rinsed. I can feel myself giving in to pleasure and losing control as she bobs her head back and forth nursing on me. I'm nearing heaven.

My ache to be inside of her gives me strength to keep from cumming in her mouth. I pull her body up and lay her facedown on the conference table. Staring at us is a picture of J. Brunson Alexander and other top Wells Fargo executives whose faces are perfectly aligned on the conference room walls. I am on a mission and those pictures are nothing more than playah hatin' voyeurs to me. I spread her legs and buttock cheeks wide, grab my dick and slowly insert myself deep into her pussy. I grab her hips for leverage as now I'm really giving it to her doggy-style. Her body tightens and freezes as she moans orgasmic pleasure with every thrust. *How you like me now?* I take half a second to look up and silently ask J. Brunson Alexander.

"Ooooo...Chris, fuck me. Don't stop baby. Don't stop." Her words turn me into an enraged jungle beast. I grunt with aggression and sweat from the heat I generate from every ram and heave. Deeper and deeper I plunge myself into her wetness, as my body yearns to satisfy this sexual hunger. I feel powerful, alive and free. My hips go on automatic pilot. Soon my rhythm of thrusts creates a tingling sensation that rules over my body as I explode with pure happiness. Everything moves in slow motion. I hear nothing. I see her face in ecstasy. I begin to lose focus. Drained of all energy, we both collapse on the table, gasping for breath.

We fall asleep on the conference table, totally oblivious to the world around us. It is 11:45 p.m. when I awake. Lissa is still in my arms feeling warm, safe and protected. The playah in me is more than satisfied, while the man silently asks questions and comes to the conclusion that this is the kind of woman I've wanted all my life. Lissa is a sweet, hardworking girl during the day and a sexy, naughty freak momma at night. She put up with all of my games of manipulation and still is willing to fulfill my fantasies. She is a soldier! I glance at her sleeping soundly, whisper, "Thank you," and gently kiss her face. This is the one.

The next day I am still feeling warm and at peace. I usually brag about my latest conquests to my homeboys, but this day is different. For the first time in a long time I truly feel...happy. Every song that I hear on my iPod reminds me of Lissa and inspires me to send her a love poem of my own:

Your beauty kisses my heart's lips
That opens and frees a sixth sense
Now I can see your sweet fragrance
Now I can hear your sunshine smiles
Now I can taste your dreams and fantasies
And if you believe in me
You will find that my love for you
Is evergreen, effervescent and everlasting

It's been three weeks and I haven't heard from Lissa. My messages to her cell phone go unreturned. Calls to her office are answered by staff saying she is traveling and unavailable. I even check with the Wells Fargo management team assigned to work with Costco but they know nothing. The next scheduled conference meeting is weeks away. I'm feeling lost and confused. Has Lissa turned the "play him, dog him" game on me?

It isn't until I receive a postcard from Spain that my questions are finally answered.

Hola Chris,

I'm sorry I haven't been in touch but I am in Barcelona on my honeymoon. Brunson and I got married and I really have you to thank for helping me to become a new woman—a woman ready and willing to take chances. You gave me the confidence to be who I always wanted to be. A woman my husband adores! By the way, the sangria here in Spain is even better! Good luck to you.

Sincerely,
Lissa Lawton-Alexander.

Married? To Old Fucking Fuddy-Duddy? I crush the note in my hand and throw that fucker away in the trash.

Damn. The playah got played.

A ONE-DAY LUST AFFAIR

Velvet

The best thing about writing erotica is getting so excited that I have to stop and open a window!

—Velvet

Morning

The day started off like every Saturday in the month. Yori woke up at eight a.m.—for her that was sleeping late—showered, made a single cup of coffee, dressed in a blue jean skirt and white shirt and was out of the door before nine. She was the regimented type and even on the weekends adhered to a schedule.

Yori Samuels had had a tough work-week. She was the assistant principal of one of New York's worst public schools. During the course of the week, at least fifty kids had come through her office. Most of them had been brought in for fighting, carrying weapons or cursing out the teacher. Yori was looking forward to her Saturday morning ritual—shopping at Chelsea Market. Chelsea Market was a one-stop-shopping food emporium with everything from butchers to fishmongers to bakers to florists. Having quality vendors under one roof made it a consumer's oasis. It was a pleasant shopping experience with a waterfall in the center of the complex and unique stores throughout. Browsing around the shopping center relaxed Yori, and today that's exactly what she needed after her trying week.

Instead of taking the subway or a taxi, she walked the twenty-something blocks to get in her morning exercise. The market wasn't bustling with people when she arrived, which was perfect. There were only a small number of shoppers at that time of the morning, and she loved the peacefulness of the place. Yori was a private person, and didn't like crowds, so she came early to avoid the masses.

Yori's first stop was the fruit and vegetable market. She loaded up on a week's worth of freshness. Next she went to the fishmonger and bought salmon filets, tilapia, and half a pound of prawns. Before heading home, she had two more shops to visit, the butcher and the baker.

"What can I get ya?" asked the butcher wearing a blood-stained apron.

"A pound of ground sirloin, a half pound of smoked turkey, and..." Yori stopped talking when she felt someone brush against her shopping bags.

"Excuse me," said a man with deep baritone voice, smiling at her.

She looked at the guy who was standing extremely close to her, invading her personal space. He was as dark as milk chocolate, tall and lean like a GQ model. He had a killer smile and dimples that pierced his cheeks when he spoke.

Yori took three steps to her left to create some distance between them. Although he was fine as all get out, she wasn't interested in men at the moment. Her last boyfriend had broken her heart by dumping her without warning, and the memory of the breakup was still fresh in her mind.

She continued ordering, and when she finished, Yori headed out. Before she reached the door, a handle broke on one of her shopping bags, and her vegetables and fruit spilled out onto the floor. She kneeled down to retrieve the scattered produce.

"Here, let me get that," the handsome hunk said, rushing over and bending down to pick up a bright red, shining apple.

Yori looked at the ripe piece of fruit that he was holding and couldn't help but think that she was being tempted, like Eve tempted by the serpent in the Garden of Eden. She quickly took the apple. "Thanks." She gathered up her bags and raced out of the shop without looking back.

"Yo, Ma! Wait up!"

Yori stopped in her tracks. She didn't need to turn around. She knew the guy from butcher shop was coming up behind her. As his steps got closer, she could feel the hairs on the back of her neck stand at attention, and she got a tingling feeling in her legs.

"You forgot this," he said, holding up a banana. "It must have separated from the bunch."

The phallic symbol was making her wet, and she didn't know why. On second thought, she knew exactly why the banana was making her horny. It looked like a hard strong dick, something she hadn't had in months. Yori wanted to grab the banana, but she was frozen, frozen by the fine specimen of a man standing before her.

"Are you okay?" he asked, looking at her face, which was turning crimson.

Yori was feeling flushed and weak at the knees. Looking at him with the banana was turning her on, and her face betrayed her true feelings. "I think I need some food," she managed to say, instead of telling him the truth.

"Come on, let's go to the baker and get some breakfast." He took her by the arm and led her across the hall to Amy's Bread. He ordered two croissants, two cups of fresh fruit, and orange juice. He then led them to a corner table.

Yori had only had a cup of coffee before leaving home and was now starving. Although she was as hungry as a linebacker, Yori pinched small pieces off of the croissant and nibbled on the fruit. She didn't want to wolf down her meal in front of the sexy stranger. Eating slowly took a little longer, but it gave her time to check out this guy on the sly. As she ate, she cut her eyes at him, hoping that he didn't notice. She glanced at his left hand and was pleased to see that he wasn't wearing a wedding band. When she finally finished, she looked over at him and said, "Thanks, uh...what's your name?"

He smiled a dazzling smile and said, "Tony. And yours?"

"Yori."

"Lori?"

"No. Yori. It's like Lori but with a *Y.*"

"Oh, that's a pretty name for a pretty woman." He smiled again, taking in her beauty. Yori was the color of a copper penny, with reddish-brown hair she wore cut in a bob. Her eyes were almond shaped, and her lips were full and kissable. She had a natural beauty, and wore little makeup. Tony's eyes roamed the length of her body. Although she was sitting down, he could see that she had full breasts and a small waist. She wore a long skirt, so he couldn't see her legs, but what he saw was appealing. She seemed on the conservative side, and Tony found the reserved type appealing. He was a full-blooded male and didn't like aggressive women who took the chase away from the man. Yori presented a challenge and he found that alluring. His last relationship had ended a month ago, and he hadn't been laid since. He found Yori extremely attractive and wanted the chance to get to know her—in and out of the sack.

Yori felt herself blushing. She was enjoying his compliments. As much as she didn't want to admit it, it felt good being in the presence of a handsome man, instead of a bunch of unruly adolescents. "Thanks. And thanks for breakfast, but I've got to be going." Although Yori was enjoying his company, she didn't know him, and didn't usually engage strangers.

He touched her hand. "Why are you rushing off? It's Saturday."

A jolt of sexual energy surged through Yori's body the moment he made contact with her skin. She looked down at his large hand resting on top of hers and couldn't help but wonder if his hand size was an indication of his cock size. If it did, then he was packing a massive weapon. That thought alone made her clit twitch. Yori wasn't the promiscuous type; nevertheless she loved a man with a big dick.

She couldn't think of a quick lie as to why she had to rush off. The truth was that she didn't have anything else to do for the rest of the day and was a little curious as to what he had in mind. "Yes, it is Saturday, but I have things to do," she said, telling him a little white lie, not wanting to appear easy.

He took one last bite of his croissant, and then gave her hand a little squeeze. "Do you think they could wait?" Tony asked, refusing to let this fine femme get away so soon. "Come on. I want to show you something." He gathered her bags with his free hand and led her out into the hallway, into the florist next door.

Tony picked out a dozen assorted flowers—birds of paradise, purple orchids, calla lilies, gerbera daisies and pink roses—and handed them to Yori. "These are for you, beautiful." He then took her hand again and said, "Come on, let's go."

"Wait a minute." She pulled back. "You can't leave without paying for these flowers."

"Oh, yes I can. I own the place." Tony's flower shop was directly across from the butcher. He had seen her from across the hall and had immediately come over, anxious to meet the beautiful stranger.

"Wow, I would have never taken you for a florist," Yori said, looking hard as she tried to juxtapose his totally male mannerism with this surprising softer side.

"I love being surrounded by pretty things," he admitted, "which is why when I saw you, I just couldn't resist coming over to say hello."

Oh, he's smooth, Yori thought as she looked him up and down.

"See anything else you like?"

Their eyes met, and both could feel a magnetic energy drawing them together.

Yes, you! Tony was bringing out feelings in Yori that she hadn't felt in a long time, and she couldn't deny them. Yori had a secret "bad girl" side that only her ex-lovers knew about. Although her mother had been a prude and taught Yori that good girls didn't have sex out of wedlock, Yori hadn't bought into that antiquated notion and had had plenty of sex without a ring. Yori hadn't felt this way about a man in a long time. Tony's sex appeal was bringing her bad girl persona to the surface, which rarely happened. Her wild side only appeared after she was in a relationship, but today her feelings of lust for him were overpowering her sensibility. The lack of heated sex in her life was making her vulnerable to his charm.

Tony saw that she was checking him out and was glad that the flowers had softened her resolve. He used her silence to his advantage and grabbed her hand, and so they left the market, emerging into the bright sunlight.

Yori started to pull away, but the temptation to be with him was too strong to resist. She felt an excited lustfulness every time their eyes met. Yori was curious to find out what was beneath his charming smile and polite manners. The mystery of the unknown had her intrigued, and she wondered what type of lover he would be. Sex appeal oozed from every pore in his body, and she could just imagine his full lips sucking her nipples and teasing her clit. She shook her head slightly, trying to shake loose those thoughts.

They headed out of Chelsea Market together walking hand in hand, and Yori felt comfortable out in the open; besides what could happen in the broad daylight?

Afternoon

Tony was pleased that Yori was willing to spend some time with him. He had been drawn to her from the moment he laid eyes on her. He could sense that she was apprehensive and knew he had to be careful with his approach. So far, everything was gelling. They were out of the market and walking down the street. As they waited at the corner for the light to change, he squeezed her hand and then caressed her palm with his thumb. Even after they had crossed the street, he didn't let go.

Yori was surprised at herself. Here she was walking down the street holding hands with a stranger, but it felt good, as if they had known each other for years.

"Do you like browsing in antique shops?" Tony asked, breaking the silence.

"Yes, I love them."

"Good. There's a great little shop around the corner."

Yori couldn't believe that this guy liked antiques; most men hated browsing around amongst old things. Tony was getting more interesting with each passing minute.

They walked down Ninth Avenue and rounded the corner at

Fourteenth Street, which was bustling with people. He stopped at a nondescript building. "It's in here."

Yori looked at the building but didn't see any stores. There wasn't a storefront on the ground level or the second level. "Where? I don't see any stores."

"It's upstairs, on the sixth floor," he said, walking inside.

She hung back for a moment, trying to decide whether or not to go into a strange building with a strange man. Out on the street she felt safe, but she wasn't so sure about going indoors with him.

Tony noticed her hesitancy. "Don't worry. It's safe," he said, as if reading her mind.

Yori thought for a second, and decided, why not? She was already doing something outside her norm. The day had taken on a completely different spin, and she was enjoying the adventure. Tony was being the perfect gentleman, and she didn't feel threatened. "Okay," she said, and followed him inside.

The building was prewar and had a dank, dusty smell to it. The original woodwork was ornate and the hardwood floors creaked with each step they took. At the far end of a narrow hallway was an old gated elevator. Tony pulled back the gate, and Yori stepped inside. The elevator was small and they practically stood shoulder to shoulder.

She inhaled slightly and could smell his cologne, which was masculine with a hint of musk. The sexy scent was turning her on. Yori could feel a rush of excitement come over her. Being this close to Tony was turning her on and she was amazed at the urgency that she felt in her loins. The elevator stopped, bringing her out of her lusting trance.

Tony took her hand and helped her out. "It's down the hall."

Yori followed him—checking out his tight ass as he walked—until they came upon a quaint little shop. The plate-glass windows faced the hallway and were lined with antique dolls and toys. Tony opened the door, and it made creaking sounds like in an old black-and-white movie.

Inside, the store was full of dust-covered relics. There were crystal champagne glasses with monogrammed letters etched into the glass, silver tea servers, old chandeliers—even a vintage gramaphone.

Yori turned the crank to see if the turntable worked, and it did. "Wow, I've only seen these things in the movies."

"Yeah, this place has some amazing stuff."

They browsed around the store, taking in the items from yesteryear. When they finished their tour, they left and went back to the elevator. Tony slid open the gate, and then pulled it closed once they were inside. He pushed the operating lever to the left, and the elevator started to slowly descend.

Yori looked at her hands, which were covered in dust. "Oh, my hands are so dirty from touching everything."

"Being dirty isn't such a bad thing," Tony commented with an alluring twist to his lips.

Yori could only stare with curious disbelief.

He pulled his T-shirt out of his waistband. "Well, if dirty girl isn't your style, use this…" he offered, leaving the rest of his challenge unspoken.

Accepting his dare, Yori stepped closer and began rubbing her hands on his shirt. She could feel his taut stomach muscles as she rubbed.

Tony's dick began pulsating faster and faster with each touch. He stepped closer until they were nearly chest to chest. He put her bags on the floor and put his hands on top of hers. He gently guided them down to his wanting cock. Tony moved her hands in a circular motion so that she could feel his protruding bulge.

Yori swallowed hard the moment her hands landed on his

crotch. His dick was pushing against his jeans. She wanted to pull away, but his cock felt too inviting. Lust began to possess her mind and body, forcing all rational thoughts out of her mind. She started rubbing his crotch, making his cock harder and harder.

Tony reached behind him and pulled the lever to the right, causing the elevator to jolt to an abrupt stop. He then turned Yori around so that her back was to him. Tony started kissing the nape of her neck, while grinding his cock into her ass.

Yori's mind was trying to intercede, screaming, *STOP!*, but her body was screaming, *FUCK ME!* She dropped the flowers, and backed up farther into him. Temptation had taken over her body, and she was now totally possessed with lust. At the moment, Yori felt like a real dirty girl, and she liked it.

Tony lifted up her skirt, found her panties and slid them down her legs. He reached underneath her ass and started massaging her clit. He didn't stop until she started moaning in ecstasy. He eased his finger into her hole and found that she was dripping wet and ready for what he had to offer. He unzipped his pants and took out his massive dick. He bent her over so that he could have easier access, then introduced the head of his dick to her pussy lips. He rubbed the tip back and forth, teasing her, making her want him more.

"Fuck me!" Yori heard herself say in a raspy voice. She was surprised at herself and hardly recognized her own voice. It was like a seductress had invaded her body and taken over her will.

Tony didn't waste any time. He entered her with his enormous cock. Her pussy walls were warm and tight, and his dick felt right at home inside of her. He closed his eyes and began pumping in and out, in and out. He grabbed her hips and continued working.

Yori held on to the elevator walls, as he rocked her world.

He was riding her like she was a prized mare, and it felt good. Her last boyfriend had had a small dick and barely filled her up. Tony, in contrast, was giving her more beef than she could handle. Yori wanted to scream out in pleasure, but didn't. She didn't want to alarm the tenants, so she took the fuck of her life like a pro. She could feel her creamy cum oozing down her legs as she reached the verge of orgasm.

Tony pumped a few more times before cumming. He felt his army of men escaping, pulled out and jacked off in his hands. Once his cum finished spouting out of his tiny hole, he rubbed the sticky goo on his T-shirt and put his dick back in his pants. He picked up Yori's panties and helped her into them.

Yori straightened her clothes and smoothed down her hair, which had come out of place during their elevator "ride."

Tony started the elevator again, picked up her groceries and flowers and stood there like nothing had happened. When they reached the ground floor, he opened the door and led her out.

The afternoon sun greeted them the moment they stepped out of the dark building. Yori suddenly felt ashamed. It was like the sun was shedding light on her dirty little secret. She began nervously adjusting her clothes.

Tony looked at her, and he could see that she was uncomfortable and probably regretting what had just happened. He pulled her close to him. "It's all right. We didn't do anything wrong. We are consenting adults who gave into our desires. There's nothing wrong with that, is there?"

Yori looked down to the ground and back up at him. He was smiling broadly, his captivating smile causing her heart to melt. "No, there isn't."

"Come on, let's get some lunch. We've worked up an appetite." He chuckled.

Yori couldn't help but smile. They had indeed worked up an

appetite. She started to go home, but she had feasted all day on this delicious stranger, and still was far from full. "Okay," she said, curious as to what other surprises the day might bring.

Evening

Over lunch, they shared their life stories and chatted about everything from politics—they still couldn't believe that America had a black president—to global warming, to the ever changing stock market. Tony was a great conversationalist, and Yori was enjoying his company. He had made her feel at ease and didn't focus on the great sex that they had just had. After lunch, he took her to a few art galleries in SoHo. The afternoon morphed into evening, and they were still together.

"I'd better get going," Yori told him.

"Please, don't. I know this great little Latin joint not too far from here."

"The last time I went to a great little place with you, we ended up interconnected," she said, raising her eyebrows.

"Touché." He held up the palms of his hands. "I promise; no hanky-panky. It's about the music this time. You up for a little salsa dancing?"

"And you really believe that some hot, sweaty, sexy salsa dancing is going to squelch your desire for a little more hanky-panky?" Yori asked with a cunning smile.

"You know, to be a relative stranger, you already know me so well. So how about it?"

She nodded her head slowly, confirming to herself that she'd just agreed to partake in some dirty dancing. Apparently her will was no match for Mr. Tony's sexy ways.

That's all he needed to know. Tony paid the bill and gathered her belongings. They walked two short blocks to the salsa spot. Inside was small with about ten tables lining the perimeter of a tiny dance floor packed with gyrating bodies all moving to the hot and pulsating rhythms. Tony found them an empty table and immediately ordered drinks from the waitress.

Yori leaned over. "This is nice. I love this music...Celia Cruz, Tito Puente..." she said, and began humming along.

"Come on, let's dance." He reached for her hand and pulled her into the bay of scintillating dancers.

They began dancing, attempting to keep up with the frenzied stepping of the much more experienced partners. Their successes were met with smiles, their foibles with hearty laughter. Yori liked that despite their steps being out of sync, their dispositions were in step.

When the music changed, offering the couple a slower paced, *salsa romàntica* tune by Marc Anthony, Yori reached up and hugged Tony's neck, and he caressed her waist. The song was mesmerizing, putting them into a trance. Yori closed her eyes, and unable to understand the Spanish lyrics, she let go and let her body do the listening.

The sexy sounds, combined with holding this incredible woman again, were making Tony horny. He pulled Yori closer and started grinding against her pelvis.

Yori could feel Tony's ever-expanding cock and swallowed hard. As much as she didn't want to admit it, she wanted him again. He was indeed like the serpent tempting her with lust. Yori opened her eyes and looked around to see if anyone was watching them, but no one was paying them any attention. She gave in to his moves and matched them with her own. Soon, they were in a heated entanglement.

"Let's go to the back," he whispered in her ear.

Yori didn't say a word, just followed her newly minted lover.

Tony knocked on the door that said *Janitor*. When no one answered, he opened it. They went inside, and he locked it behind them. The room was tiny, only slightly larger than the lavatory on a plane.

"Take off your panties," he said, in a deep voice.

Yori complied. He then picked her up and sat her on top of the small sink. Tony dropped to his knees and began eating her out. Yori threw her head back and grabbed ahold of his head to balance herself.

Tony explored the petals of her juicy pussy with his tongue, sucking her clit, and jetting his tongue in and out of her. Once he brought her to climax, he started to enter her, but she stopped him.

"I want to taste that big dick of yours." Yori was doing and saying things that she had never done before. She had never wanted to suck a cock until now. Although she had performed oral sex before, she didn't enjoy it, but for some reason, she wanted to put her lips around Tony's rock-hard penis.

Before trading positions, Yori looked in the old rusted mirror and stared at Tony's cock. The sight of his thick long dick was making her salivate. She then took it in her hands, and watched the reflection of herself stroking his lethal weapon.

"Hey, open up in there!! I need to use the can!" a voice from the other side of the door yelled.

Tony and Yori heard the man, but didn't stop their foreplay. They were in a zone and didn't care about the world beyond the tiny closet.

"He'll find the right room eventually," Tony whispered in her ear.

Yori nodded her head in agreement. No stranger's need could be as urgent as hers at the moment.

The man banged on the door a couple of times but stopped once he realized he had the wrong door.

Once she finished her hand job, she kneeled down on the tiny floor and began sucking Tony off with abandon. Her mouth made love to his dick as if her life depended on it. She was sucking so hard that she could taste precum oozing out of his dick. The sweet, salty taste was like an aphrodisiac turning her on even more. She wanted to suck all of his cum out and continued bobbing her head, applying pressure with her mouth.

"Damn, baby, that feels so good."

Tony was on the verge of cumming but didn't want to explode in her mouth. He extracted himself and came in the sink.

Now that they had gotten the lustful monkey off their backs, they went back to their seats feeling totally satisfied. They could have stayed holed up in the closet all night, but they figured evidently more patrons would come banging on the door.

They stayed for two sets, before heading out.

"Can I get you a taxi?" Tony offered.

"Yes, that would be nice."

He stepped to the curb and raised his arm, trying to flag down a cab. Once the taxi came, he helped her inside and then asked for her phone number. They exchanged numbers and promised to keep in touch.

As Yori rode home, she thought about the unexpected events of the day. This day had been like no other, and she felt liberated. Tony had broken down all of her sexual inhibitions. In a matter of hours, he had taught her to give in to her temptations and live for the moment.

She had thought that this day would be like every other Saturday, but she was wrong. It had been far better than she could have ever imagined. Her one day of lust was something that she would remember for years to cum!

PARTY OF FOUR

BLACK

The sexiest vacation spot? My house.

—BLACK

There were the moments between night and dawn when the sky hadn't completed the transition, and the stars were twinkling their final curtain call.

Debby Ericson lay awake watching the last dots fade from the horizon, listening to the even rhythm of her husband's breathing, and she knew from the even tempo he was still dreaming, in color. She smiled as she rolled from beneath the down comforter, her toes touching the retro shag rug. Heat curled around her ankles, and a relieved sigh escaped her plump lips. The new furnace was definitely working.

Scooting back on the bed, she looked over her shoulder at the man she'd loved for the majority of her life. He'd given her two incredible children, had worked menial jobs right after college so that she could stay home with their daughters, then had encouraged her to pursue her own career after their girls had begun school. When all of their friends were trading in their spouses for newer models, she and Mark had locked their doors and opened their hearts to one another. Mark had loved her since they were in middle school, and he could take her to sexual heights she had never achieved with anyone else; even her own hands were incapable of satisfying the ache that throbbed constantly in the deepest parts of her.

If he weren't sleeping, Debby would have had him then, but his job as CEO of Carrollton Trucking Company was demanding and often required sixteen-hour days.

They would play tonight. He was getting off early, he'd told her yesterday.

They were the perfect, somewhat understated, definitely misinterpreted, middle- to upper-class black family. Very straight laced—according to those in the community. Mark was the white-collar executive who had an interior decorator as a wife, but behind the triple-locked, rustic wood, French-styled front doors they were freaky, nudist, hedonists who were secretly contemplating their next big adventure. Over the years they'd learned that sex with partners outside their marriage kept the excitement going inside their marriage. Over the years they'd been with a few people, and their bond had only grown stronger.

A thrill danced down Debby's thighs, and she welcomed the beginning of a microclimax. Just thinking about the things they'd done in the past made her want to play dress-up right then, dive beneath the covers and have her way with Mark.

The New Year had begun less than ten months ago, and to indulge Mark's fantasies, she'd dressed up as a waitress, nurse, teacher, prison guard, slutty office temp, flight attendant, package delivery woman and cougar. After the cougar fantasy, he'd given her two-carat, diamond stud earrings. He'd loved the wig with the gray streak in the front.

As often as once a week, she found fantasy suggestions—taped to her computer mouse, coffee cup, toothbrush, mirror and thong drawer—as to which woman he wanted greeting him when he locked their bedroom door that night.

Debby ran her hand up the inside of her thigh and found wetness. She was always charged with sexual energy that had him just a thought away all day, every day.

Debby could honestly say she was sincerely, happily in love. Their nest was empty for the first time in twenty years, their oldest child studying abroad, and their youngest daughter happily acclimated at Temple University.

They wouldn't be parents again until fall break, and the girls knew better than to come home unannounced. Their dad had taken care of that over their weekly webcam call last weekend.

Debby suppressed a giggle. His loving but firm stance had turned her on. Remembering how she'd screwed Mark's brains out in every room except their daughters' made her want him again, but his breathing hadn't changed. He would be asleep for another hour.

Gently she slid her hand down his shoulder to the top of the cover. In his sleep, Mark moved closer to her side of the bed, and she couldn't resist climbing back under the covers to be enveloped in his love. He encircled her and his hands rubbed up and down her arms while he settled his chin between her shoulder blades. His slow exhale spread across her bare back. He was finally awake.

Debby curved her body and he curled around her. The love between them was gentle yet powerful, like a hug.

"I dreamed in color," he told her, growling like a bear as he pulled her to him.

"You're color blind," she informed him, smiling at the irony.

"God has a sense of humor." She could feel his finger at the crack of her behind, and in a deft movement, he peeled off her thong. "What color is this?" He dragged it up beneath the covers and rubbed it against her breasts. Debby was one of those women whose nipples had their own story to tell. When aroused, they stood out an inch, like pencil erasers. Unaroused, they were dots on a map waiting to be recognized.

She didn't bother to look at the thong dangling from his finger. "Red."

He flicked his wrist and sent the garment onto the floor, kissing her back deeply with his tongue, sending thrills down her buttcrack to her clit, which seemed to vibrate.

"I love red. It's the color of passion," he said, as her body responded. He hadn't always been color blind.

Her muscles loosened, and her legs wanted to welcome him, but she loved playing hard to get early in the morning. Intentionally she crossed her legs and drew them up behind her, knowing he liked to work a little before he actually left for work. He enjoyed the tease as much as the win.

In the distance, the first birds began to awaken and call to one another. Soon, she and Mark would be in their respective cars heading to work in opposite directions. She pushed the thoughts away and let the beauty of the moment fill in all the spaces.

"Are you going to work today?" Her voice was husky as she tempted him. They could call in sick together. He bit her back, causing her to arch, her legs loosening just a little. He pushed at them, pretending to wrestle with her.

"Why? You got a boyfriend coming by that I don't know about?"

A giggle started in her chest, as she scooted back toward his naked body. "Yes. His name is Dexter, and he's got a much bigger dick than you."

"Does he really now?" Mark bit her shoulder and she moaned, clutching the fitted sheet. He was claiming his possession and she loved it. He knew better than anyone how she liked to be pleased. His tongue found the most sensitive spot on the back of her neck and when she squirmed, he palmed her 34DDs and massaged until her nipples were at their fullest.

Breathless, she crawled across the bed, as if to get away.

"Dexter's dick is rather huge, darling. I can't lie here playing with you all day. I have to plan his birthday."

Debby held her breath. Mark's fortieth birthday was a big deal, but he didn't seem to care what he did this year. She'd been agonizing for months about what to do and he had ruled out just about everything, including traveling. They'd just returned from a trip to Japan three weeks ago, and Mark didn't want to go anywhere until after President's Club, the company trip in January.

She'd booked, then canceled, a room at the Mansion, an exclusive hotel on Peachtree Street in the heart of Atlanta's swank hotel district. They had their house all to themselves and were very comfortable being home. With their college reunion the following weekend, Mark had already said he didn't want to go away, knowing they were committed to attending that event.

"I'm calling Dexter. He wants to fuck me good," she teased.

Mark pulled Debby by her ankle, then reached till his fingers greeted her wetness. Debby couldn't help but tighten her vaginal muscles and clutch them. Mark made her feel so good.

"So wet," he whispered.

"Mmm."

The sky had turned a dusty navy blue and looked so lovely she didn't want to close her eyes, but the pleasure was so great, she wanted to capture it in her heart and imprint it in her memory bank. Her love for Mark was passionate and deeply poignant. She would do anything for him.

Debby lay on her stomach while Mark finger-fucked her. He bit her hip and she yelped and squeezed her buttcheeks, laughing. "You're driving me insane, Mark Dexter Ericson."

"What does Dexter want for his birthday?" he asked, loving his alter ego. Lying on his side, his hand moving inside of her, his breath glided across the hump of her backside.

"I don't know. I thought about surprising him. He loves surprises, unlike you, darling. Speaking of which, Anya from college called yesterday. She and Mario are coming for the reunion next week."

Debby turned to see her husband's face. The pleasure and surprise had a positive effect on him. And he was eye-level with her ass.

"It's been over twenty years. How are they?" his strokes became long and deeper.

She spread her legs a little more. "Fine. I insisted they stay with us while they're here. No need for them to rent a hotel room when we have the guest house."

"That was nice of you, Mrs. Ericson." The tempo of his finger-fucking had changed and he was hitting her G-spot just right each time. At the same time, he caressed her bottom, her second most sensitive erogenous zone. The combination of the two had a dizzying effect on her. However, part of pleasing her was to please him. Debby considered moving, but one look at his face told her he was pleased.

"You think they might like a repeat of our foursome? That night was hot. *Really* hot." Mark's voice was naturally deep, but it now took on a sensual quality that caused a thrill to shimmy up her already stimulated backside. Debby sighed.

"As a matter of fact, Anya hinted strongly that she and Mario would be open to a repeat performance."

"Did she now?"

Mark's fingers plunged into her deeply. Debby couldn't widen her legs any farther. She dropped her cheek to the sheet and moved her hips in rhythm to his hand.

"So a repeat isn't out of the question?" he said, before licking her butt.

"Oh, Mark..." More words refused to come and Debby didn't care. The thought of their friends coming to their house made her reach for Mark and kiss him hard. A night of illicit passion once every twenty years sounded just perfect to her. Debby ground her hips against his hand, and she clutched his hand to her lips.

"You're sexy as hell, baby." Mark sighed, his hand leaving her delicate folds. As soon as he parted from her, she wanted to become one with him again, but he was ahead of her and climbed onto her back, their knees meeting, his sex falling between her butt and thighs. His chest met her back and he pressed his weight into her the way she liked, as their fingers curled together.

For a few seconds, their hands were linked and her love grew tighter, stronger. The pulsing intensified between her legs, and she said nothing, basking in the bond of this single moment of Mark and silence and dawn.

Their bodies melded, but didn't join and she loved the togetherness, the anticipation growing like fire inside of her.

Debby had to admit the idea of reuniting their foursome had pushed her to the brink of climax. They'd had the best time way back when, but she and Mark had never repeated the experience with Anya and Mario, not wanting to ruin the memory.

Speaking to Anya yesterday had brought back memories of their shared weekend and of how the freak in her had awakened.

They'd lost an eight ball in the corner pocket shot to the guys and had to French kiss. The next loss, the bras had to come off, nipples became fair game, and the rest was history. Now all she wanted was them. All of their hands on her body, their mouths, their fingers, their smiles bathing her in pleasure.

Mark's voice brought her back to reality and lovemaking.

"That would be a nice birthday present," he whispered into her ear. His hands surged through her short stylish haircut, his mouth devouring her back and shoulders.

She turned to take his swollen dick in her hand and stroked him. "You sure you want that as your gift?"

His dark eyes danced as his mouth found her nipple. "I have everything else I want."

Pulling Debby to him, he plunged into her and she gasped before a guttural sound fought out of her. Their coupling was hungry and rough. His arm crossing her body, he thrust hard and deep.

She turned to gaze into his eyes and could see the determination and purpose. Mark wanted to leave his impression on her for the rest of the day. He wanted to give her something to think about when her clients were talking glass dining room tables, slate flooring or tile, wallpaper or paint. He wanted her to think about getting fucked by her husband this morning.

Her climax began to curl in her toes, and she tightened her vaginal wall muscles. Mark bit her ear. He wasn't ready to come, but she didn't care. She couldn't control the climax riding up her legs on the coattails of love. "Come with me, baby," she begged him.

His thrusts were the most intense her body could withstand. Raking him with her nails was her final chord to a refrain that had ended perfectly. She burst. Her mouth flew open and her body sailed into the pink and purple dawn as he finally filled her.

* * *

Mark's actual birthday had come and gone. They had celebrated for more than a week with Mark going in late every day. Debby had gotten used to being with him all week in the mornings, sharing breakfast and talking. But when he had to go in for an early meeting this morning, she had pouted, until she found the red box with her name written in Mark's familiar script, left on the seat of her BMW.

Mark had bought her something, but what? And why? Anya and Mario—his birthday presents—were arriving today. It was his day to receive gifts.

Tossing her briefcase onto the seat, she climbed into the car and lifted the lid on the box. Inside was the diamond emerald bangle bracelet that she'd been eyeing while they'd been in Japan. It had been too much yen, and she'd walked away from it, but he'd bought it anyway behind her back.

Smiling, she leaned her head on the steering wheel then sat up, wondering how she'd gotten so lucky. The bracelet was gorgeous, but it wasn't just the jewelry. Mark was the most amazing man, and he was going to get it good tonight. She pressed the phone button inside the steering wheel that dialed his phone.

"Did you get your present?" he asked immediately.

"You know I did. How did you do this without me knowing?"

"I had to be very sneaky. But let me tell you why. I did it because you indulge my every fantasy and my every whim. Before our company arrives tomorrow, I wanted you to know that I love you. I'm going to have a good time with Anya and Mario, but I didn't want you to think this is some kind of consolation prize for my birthday present."

"Oh, Mark," she breathed, as she slipped on her bracelet. "I love you, but you know me better than that."

"I do, but you're still a woman. And that is a nice bracelet. It's for you, my love."

She sighed slowly, smiling, looking at the dazzling emeralds. "I love it."

"Good. Look on the backseat."

"What?" Debby spun around and saw the small box from her favorite exclusive lingerie store. She pulled up the black and gold box and untied the string. Inside were two beige camouflage thongs.

"Are these for me?"

"Yes, for you and Anya. My only request. I'd like to at least see your lingerie once in a while."

"No problem. I know camouflage is about the only color you can see, so I will make sure you get an eyeful. And, darling, I do everything I do because I love seeing you happy. We're going to have a great time tomorrow."

"We are, aren't we? Two clits, four breasts, an extra dick... I've got to stop thinking about it or I won't be able to leave my office."

Just like that, he woke up her clit, which *would* distract her all day. "It's going to be amazing. I'll see you tonight."

"Don't work too hard," Mark said.

"Bye, darling," she said, and blew him a kiss.

"Four breasts, two clits, two dicks. You said that, didn't you, honey? Tell the truth, Mark." Debby and Anya stood on one side of the billiard table in the play room, as she and Mark playfully referred to the thousand-foot recreation and theater room in their home.

Mark and Mario were down to their boxers, looking only slightly uncomfortable, considering that the girls were only out of their shoes and jewelry and just had two balls left on the table.

"I don't recall that conversation, sweetheart."

"You're such a fibber," Debby told him, chuckling as she leaned down, giving them an eyeful. She held her pose and drew the pool stick back. Slowly she rotated the cue between her fingers and pumped it, still not striking the white ball, loving that she'd decided early on to go braless. "Six, corner pocket." The shot dropped without a problem.

"Great shot, partner." Anya walked by, braless as well.

Supper had long been eaten and they had all moved on to after-dinner drinks and seduction. The couple had arrived only a few hours ago and it was like the twenty years between visits had just slipped away.

Playing strip billiards again had been Mario's idea, and it was the perfect ice-breaker. Catching up had taken most of the evening, but now everyone was comfortable, except for Mark who had sprouted a tent in the front of his boxers. He was hot for Debby, but Anya's round ass was doing something to him as well. His cock had radar for her.

Debby gazed at Mario, openly admiring his physique. He'd stayed in excellent physical shape. The commentator for a popular sports channel, he was a dark chocolate dreamboat, with a buzzed haircut, his grin worth a million bucks, while Anya reminded Debby of the model Roshumba.

She'd become an executive vice president for a major hotel chain. They had four children, but they'd left their brood back in Philadelphia to come to Atlanta for the reunion and to recreate a night of passion.

"I thought the reunion started tonight," Mario complained good-naturedly. "I'm supposed to be getting drunk with people I don't remember. Not with you two losers," he said to Anya and Debby.

The girls laughed. "We're not the ones standing around in

our drawers," Debby told Mario as she handed him his Hennessey and Coke. She giggled like a schoolgirl when he pulled her in for a kiss on the cheek that slowly turned into more.

Mario had a lot going for him, including a large dick that Debby hadn't forgotten. When they broke apart, her lips tingled from the feel of another man's lips. Then she leaned over and kissed her husband. The different and familiar were the best of both worlds.

Anya watched the byplay. "Eight ball, right center." She took aim at the last ball on the table for the women and tapped it in, ending the game. She undid the belt from her waist and let it slip to the floor, peeled off the silk sweater and it landed on the floor too. Her breasts were bare and lovely. "Honey, this is the *cock and tail* party I want to be at. We'll reunite with the others tomorrow for the dinner." Anya winked at Mario. "This place has way better towels, so—" She wiggled four fingers, while mouthing four to him.

Everyone burst out laughing. "You two are nuts." Mark told them, sliding all of the pool cues onto the table before reaching for Anya.

"It's her. She's got me acting like a kid." Mario reached out and gave Anya a sensual kiss.

"Well, they earned their reward," Mark told Mario. "I guess we owe them their wish to see us go first."

The girls walked ahead of them, their arms sliding around each other's waists.

Inside, they undressed and climbed into the king-size bed, the men in the center.

For a second Debby wondered if there would be any awkwardness between them, but there wasn't. Mario reached for Mark and they shared a kiss that was gentle yet exciting. Mario was darker than Mark, his musculature a little larger, but

Mark was taller and leaner, his dick jutting out as if to find its intended target.

The women were behind each other's husbands, watching them. Debby stroked Mario's strong arms, her mouth seeking his neck. She found the curve with her tongue, tracing up and down, seeing how good Anya had it every night. He groaned. "I like that," he said, and she moved to his ear, letting her tongue titillate until she felt his movements becoming more aggressive. She didn't want to go too far, because she wanted Mark to experience his full birthday present.

Mark's hand had left Mario's side and was now gripping Anya's thigh and she urged it around, but he wouldn't let go. He pulled her around until she was facing his penis, and he lovingly cupped her head. "Will you?"

Anya wanted him badly. Opening her mouth, she took him in as she felt her own legs being moved apart and her friend Debby lapping at her nectar. It didn't take much to set Anya off. Sucking on Mark with his wife between her legs was enough to send her into orbit. She could feel herself being pulled up on the bed and her breasts being sucked, but then she saw Mario move down between Mark's legs to take her place. She and Mark were at the top of the bed and he held her. "I always thought you had the most beautiful nipples."

"I'll come again if you suck them just right."

"I'll come if he sucks me just right," he said, watching Mario go after his dick.

"I wanna come too," Debby said, leaving Mario's dick and crawling up on the bed.

Mark lay flat on the bed, leaving Anya's nipples for a second. "Climb up here, baby."

Debby sat on his face and Anya kissed her breasts, massaging her arms and back and ass. She stimulated Mark with her nails and hands, letting them roam his body, licking him, biting Mario's nipples, letting her fingers play in his hair.

Mark's thrusts into Mario's mouth became more forceful and Debby raked his nipples, seeing how much he liked watching Anya sexing her, the sensation of his dick being sucked, and his nipples being stimulated as he ate her pussy. Finally, he burst. The first shot hit Mario in the mouth, the rest flew onto the bed. Debby went off, too, her husband licking her to completion before Mario grabbed Debby and entered her, his dick wide and full, his thrusts hard and fast.

Anya pinched Debby's nipples, and the pleasure and pain sent Debby flying. Just when she didn't think she could take any more, Mark sucked another climax out of her clit that had her screaming before the four of them collapsed in happy exhaustion.

Awakening to the patter of rain against the rooftop, Debby turned over and realized she'd just had the best foursome sex of her life. Carefully, she climbed over Anya and scooted down in front of Mark. Softly, she called his name. His eyes slid open. "Yes, dear?" He kissed the tip of her nose and brought her close to him.

"I'm starving."

"Me too," Anya said.

Mark grinned at his wife, who caressed the hairs on his chin.

"Feed your women." Playfully Debby bit him.

The ladies started giggling, and Mario's feet hit the floor with a smack. "Last one dressed is buying."

There was a lot of pushing and shoving and Debby was last to get out of bed. She followed her husband into the shower and when the car backed down the driveway, it was understood that Mark was going to pay.

* * *

"Party of four, for Ericson. This way, please." Anya and Debby clasped hands and shared private smiles as they followed Janice to their table at Scope, a quiet restaurant in Atlanta.

Brunch was filled with talk of careers and family, life in Atlanta versus Philadelphia and colleges for their respective children. Soon the meal came to an end, and they all decided to top it off with a Mimosa toast.

Seated with a view of the lake, they watched the sunlight dance off the surface of the water. "When shall we repeat our weekend party of four?" Anya asked, taking Mario's hand.

Mark kissed the back of Debby's hand, the diamonds on her new emerald bracelet sparkling. "Twenty years," Mark offered confidently. "It's worked perfectly up until now."

Everyone looked around and agreed.

Mario kissed Anya intimately. "Next time we're hosting," she said.

Late that night, warmly ensconced in their bed, Mark held his wife who he'd just made passionate love to. "You sure you don't want to see them more often?"

Debby shook her head, looking at her husband, love surrounding them. "No. I had a great time, but this was about your birthday, so I'm happy with seeing them in twenty years. I've got what I want right here. I love you, Mark."

"I love you, Debby."

Their lips met in a sensual kiss that sparked a fire that burned long into the night.

WET

Elise Gower

I think great erotica is like a fabulous dream. You should be carried away from all your sensibilities and be open to experiencing new ones.

—Elise Gower

Adrienne Corley sat in her corner office, tapping her finger against the high-tech keyboard trying to open her unrelenting schedule. She was, as usual these days, oblivious to the swirl of activity on the trading floor just outside her door. How had things gotten so far out of control? How had she already reached this one birthday that would take her smack dab into middle age? This couldn't be all there was to her life. There had to be something more.

There are about a hundred ways of dealing with a midlife crisis. Fast, expensive foreign cars and insatiable, hot young women came to mind. That's great for the guy trying to get his 007 on, but what if you're a woman—a black woman? Black women aren't supposed to be swept up in crisis, midlife or otherwise. We don't have the time.

Go with a younger man? Not likely, unless you are in deep cheddar and don't care that you'll have to finance the whole damn thing. Wealthy older man? Hell no, because for women like Adrienne, all you'll get is the old. Old *and* rich want the twentysomething girls, not REAL women knocking down forty's door. Damn! This whole mired-in-midlife-muck thing had snuck up on her, and Adrienne didn't like surprises. She lived her highly demanding life in tight order, managing the people and things around her and making them work to her satisfaction. Control was the secret to her success.

But this gnawing discontent was growing stronger every day and beginning to disrupt her well-oiled machine of a life. She was going to have to stop shoving it aside and deal with it. But how? And when? Running the sales and trading floor for a small but profitable boutique investment firm left her very little time to do anything other than eat, sleep, exercise (to maintain her alpha-female status) and work. She needed time to regroup and figure out how to get back control of her life.

It seemed the only option that made sense was to finally use some of the vacation time she'd accumulated over the years for some sort of total getaway. Yes, a trip complete with exotic venues and nonstop adventure. Maybe if she went hiking in the Himalayas she could eat and exercise and become enlightened as to why, despite nearly four decades of living, she had little of what really mattered to show for it. No husband, no kids, and, to be honest, not even the career she'd envisioned for herself. Just a high-paying job on Wall Street that saw to the bills and kept her busy during the day.

STOP! Adrienne tried to clear her mind of the pitiful and refocus on the possible. Maybe a walk around the trading floor

would help. She slipped on her Manolos, got up and headed out
of her corner office to check on her staff. That's when she noticed the screensaver on her assistant's desk. Was that Jada...on
a surfboard?

That girl really has lost her mind, she thought, but the image
stuck with her.

When she got home that night, she put on a little Mary J
and stretched out on her overstuffed sofa. She was cracking the
latest issue of *O Magazine* to check out the Halle Berry profile,
when...WHAT? Halle, in the photo spread, was working a surfboard and looking nothing like forty. Maybe there was a message in this. According to the article, the hottest surfing school
around was in Cabo San Lucas, Mexico. The five-star resort,
with a surfing school right there on the premises, sounded perfect. Maybe this was just what she needed. So despite an intoler-
ance for the unknown, the fact that she had bathing suits older
than the average surfer dude, and her concern that even the best
of weaves might not stand up to a gnarly wave, Adrienne picked
up the phone and made plans toward the sun and away from the
familiar. She was going to Cabo, to the Sonrisa Surfing School.
Hell, if Jada and Halle could do it, so could she!

Trying to make it through the last hour of an insufferable layover
in Houston, Adrienne put away her book and put all her attention into being part of the world around her instead of her usual
act of disappearing in plain sight. Observing her fellow travel-
ers, it was apparent that only two types went to Cabo—and neither was middle-aged sista. Blonde boys with perfect teeth and
starry-eyed honeymooners filled the waiting area. One couple
was so caught up in the rapture, Adrienne wondered if they
would just say the hell to everyone else and fuck each other right
there at the gate.

Both looked to be in their twenties, and the lust that radiated from them burned hotter than any Mexican sun. DAMN! Right before her eyes, with no regard for who might be watching, the man slipped his hand under the woman's skirt and began moving it in an in-and-out motion. He was clearly hitting some hot spot exactly the right way because a moan escaped her lips as she threw her head back, arched her back and lifted her pussy to meet his caress. She turned in, brushing her hand against his crotch, and whispered something in his ear that caused him to grunt, his swelling dick fighting the restriction of his shorts.

Disgusted, but at the same time aroused, Adrienne found herself entranced by their bold display. She couldn't imagine being so out there. Adrienne felt her breath catch and she quickly looked away. She felt a tightening between her own legs as heat began to radiate from her clit. Adrienne was embarrassed to be so easily aroused. Her nipples strained against her practical bra. It had been more than a year since she'd had sex with anyone other than her right hand. She'd just been too busy (and maybe too judgmental) for men in her life. She exhaled slowly but found little comfort in her effort to center herself.

"This will be the final boarding call for flight four-seven-eight-two to Cabo San Lucas," a voice announced. Grateful for the distraction, Adrienne found her ticket, looked at it hopefully and crossed the Jetway to settle into a first-class seat paid for by more business trips than she cared to tally. She fell into a fitful sleep, fighting with the two waiting area lovers in her head to keep their lewd acts to themselves and allow her some rest.

A funny, little man approached her as she waited for her bags, bearing a sign that misspelled her name. "*Señora* Corley?" he asked her expectantly, "I am Eduardo from the Sonrisa Surfing Club. I've been sent to meet you. Is there *mas* luggage?"

Adrienne began to wonder what she had gotten herself into. He was short and on the pudgy side. His unkempt, jet black hair hung bowl-like just over his ears. Eduardo stood in stark contrast to Adrienne's image of a hot and sexy surfer dude.

"There's one more bag," she said to Eduardo, nodding her head toward the baggage claim carousel. "I'll wait in the car."

"*Sí*," Eduardo responded, pointing her toward an open-air Jeep she was not at all sure about. She swung herself into the front seat, as the backbench was a mess of sand and surfboards. With no seat belt in evidence, she reached out to hold the side of her door with one hand and the roll bar overhead with the other. The Jeep lurched under the weight of her other bag as Eduardo swung it on top of the pile behind her, before starting off with a violent rumble.

The desolate roads from the airport into town churned a virtual sandstorm around her, making her wonder if this guy could even see where he was going. She held her breath and shielded her eyes as best she could. Finally they pulled onto a long, dusty road that wound closer to the beach.

A gasp escaped her lips. Before her, completely magical in its beauty, lay the Sea of Cortez. Framed by a perfect sunset, impossibly blue waves with brilliant whitecaps rushed to greet her, barely obscuring menacing black rocks jutting up from all over.

"If I could look at that every day, I might be a different person," she said to no one in particular. And in a completely uncharacteristic manner, she began to feel herself relax.

"What are those little puffs of white that keep appearing way out there?" she asked Eduardo.

"Whales, *Señora*. It is their season for mating. You picked a *muy interesante* time to come here. The sea is most alive *en esta*, ah, season."

They finally drove through a large brick gate and entered the resort. It was beautiful beyond anything she had even imagined. Flowers hung from above, as well as all around her. The scents intoxicated her.

"Wow," she said blithely.

She was shown to a beautiful *casita*, a small cottage that overlooked the resort below. Beyond it spread a rocky beach. As her host explained all of the activities that awaited her, Adrienne found herself nodding without hearing a word. Exhausted by the travel, all she wanted to do was enjoy the small meal that had been set out for her on the balcony, unpack and go to bed.

After placing the last toiletry neatly by her sink, Adrienne indulged herself with a nightcap on the balcony. She sipped it slowly, leaning over the rail, watching the brown, hard-bodied surfers-in-residence relaxing on the beach below. Her body, still feeling the residual of arousal from the airport peep show, demanded satisfaction. She told herself no, as her mind began to fantasize. But her disobedient legs spread open and let the warm breeze tease her pussy, imaging one of the men below blowing soft kisses there. She tried to resist what had become an inappropriate habit she considered completely beneath her. But once she could be sure they couldn't see her, she allowed her hand to roam her soft, brown skin and find its familiar place around the soft bush between her legs.

Teasing her clit, she let herself imagine her lover's tongue probing her and felt herself surge with desire. Squeezing her eyes tight, she allowed him to guide her hand to the places that set her on fire. And that's when she heard the voice in her ear, from somewhere out at sea. As it whispered soft and seductive demands, she let her phantom lover work the slippery wetness of her hungry snatch. She worked herself slowly at first, but the voice drove her to a greater urgency. She pushed her fingers inside herself, continuing to knead her clit with her thumb. Her other hand pulled at her aroused nipples, pinching and twisting them, finding pleasure in the pain. She began to see colors flash before her eyes as she exploded into a breathless, shivering orgasm.

Damn, she thought, more than a little embarrassed by her behavior. She checked the men below her again to make sure that she hadn't been noticed, shook her head to clear it and went to bed. But she couldn't get that voice out of her mind.

"Buenos días, Señora!" Eduardo called brightly as he met Adrienne the next morning after breakfast in the reception area. "We are ready to surf, no?"

Eduardo had stuffed his pudgy frame into enormous board shorts. Adrienne's well-toned nearly six-foot frame could still catch eyes, despite her purposely boring one-piece suit. She walked over to Eduardo with a false confidence to cover the growing fear inside her. Her hair was pulled back into the tightest bun she could manage. It was beginning to occur to her that she might not have any control down here, at all.

"You DO know I've never done this before, right?" she told Eduardo, staring out over huge, crashing surf.

"No worry, *Señora.* We no surf here. This is the time of *Xocicolto.* We drive to a special beach for you today."

"What is *SHO-she-COLT-o?*" she asked. "Some kind of *el Niño* thing?"

"No. *Xocicolto* was the son of a great *Azteca* king. I tell you more on the way there. You will like it *mucho.* I promise you, *mucho.*"

Eduardo lifted two huge surfboards as if they were simple two-by-fours and hoisted them onto the back of the jeep. Adrienne reassumed her position in the passenger seat and held on for dear life. To take her mind off the rough ride, she prodded Eduardo for more about *Xocicolto*.

"*Sí, Señora*. He was the son of a *muy, muy grande* king de *los Aztecas*. But he *no* was a good son. He was too much with *la tequila y los fiestas, comprende*? He was *muy fuerte*. Strong, you know? And he had *muy, muy* women because it was said he had special powers with them. No man's wife was safe from *Xocicolto*. Now, the king was so sad that his *hijo* was not a better man, so he told him he would give him only *uno* year to prove himself worthy to take over and lead their people. If he could not do this, the king would sacrifice him to their gods and adopt a new boy to be his prince. Well, this made *Xocicolto* afraid. But how could only a young prince do this? Well the gods knew that inside, *Xocicolto* was good. To give him the chance to please his father, they blew violent winds into the Sea of Cortez. The wind was so strong that it pushed huge rocks into the water and pushed all the greatest animals from across the sea into this one place. This angry sea threatened to wipe away the village where *los Aztecas* lived, unless one who was brave came to them. *Xocicolto* heard the call of the gods and knew that this was his time, *si*? He walked down to the beach and stood against the *grande* waves, the thunder and the lightning and the hard rain. He removed all his beautiful, precious clothing and jewels. His jewels became the shells we find on the beach. His clothing became the colorful flowers that grow there. He then stretched his arms out wide and raised his head up to meet the gods. A ray of *el sol* opened between the dark clouds to shine on him and led him on a path into the sea. As he disappeared into the sea, the surf around him calmed, and soon the sea sent wide, gentle waves to the shore. The waves are big enough to carry a man but also gentle enough to carry him without harm. *Xocicolto* only happens *uno* time each year.

When the rest of the sea is wild with wind and creatures, the part where *Xocicolto* walked is the *perfecto*. The perfect place for you to learn."

The story had been just long enough to see her to their destination. Indeed, when Adrienne looked ahead, she could see their road open onto a cove with what she had to admit was a most beautiful beach. They unloaded the car, and after a short surfing instruction on the beach with Eduardo, he placed her on her board in the water and pulled her into the brine.

As he guided her out, he continued to tell her what to expect. What she had not expected was the way it felt to ride prostrate across the living sea. Though she tried to hang on to the board, the rolling waves created undulations that took her body by surprise. She tried to focus on Eduardo's instruction and not the sensations created by having something long and hard moving under her. She remembered her embarrassment from the night before and told herself to keep it clean.

"*Señora*, I will be behind you when the waves come. When the right wave is here I will push you, but you must paddle, paddle, paddle *con* your arms like I show you on *la playa*—I mean, the beach, *sí*?"

At that moment, a large but surprisingly gentle wave crashed across the front of them. As it splashed over Adrienne's head and down her back, she heard a voice say, *In my hands, your body feels like the ripe flesh of a delectable mango—succulent and juicy.*

"Eduardo? WHAT?" she asked, more than a little alarmed.

"*Señora? Que hace?* What happened?"

"I thought I heard you..."

"No, I no say nothing."

Eduardo turned his attention back to piloting his student to an advantageous point facing the beach. Soon another large yet gentle wave washed over her, this time from behind. She could feel it first tickle her toes with a warm surf, then work its way up the back of her thighs, between her legs and over her back. As the water passed her ears, so did the voice.

I will make you open for me...then I will taste your goodness.

Despite her strong will otherwise, the suggestion caused her nipples to swell. Or was it fear, as Adrienne heard a stronger surf building behind her? The sound built as it grew closer, louder and louder as it drew upon her.

"*Señora!*" Eduardo called excitedly. "*Señora* this is it! Remember I push you and you paddle. When you feel the wave take you, you try to stand up."

The first crumbly water of the surf began to gather at her sides. As it rushed past her, the sound grew louder, completely drowning out Eduardo's encouragements. Then she felt his strong push, paddled madly, and the wave began to take her.

Feel my desire wash over you, she heard the voice say.

She felt her board lift with the crest of the wave and drive her forward with a speed that blew her hair away from her face. Too unnerved by the voice in her head to let go of the sides of her board, she held on to the surfboard as the back of the wave again tickled her toes. An unnatural warmth inside the wave's curl seemed to reach around her, grasp at her waist and pin her to the board. A surge of cool water worked its way between her and the board, filling the front of her swimsuit. A caress of the swirling currents teased her clitoris as the board's vibration banged rhythmically between her legs. A second wave cresting next to her crossed over her, encasing her in an azure tube of heat and light that turned her board over and over again. She felt one breast free itself from her suit. The cool water pulled against it as the board continued to turn, sucking mightily against her hard, erect nipple. She couldn't scream for fear of taking in water, and she couldn't stop herself from going with the ecstasy she felt growing inside her. Hanging on, unable to let go lest she lose this sensation, she felt the second wave passing her with a great roar. She was unnerved and confused and still unsatisfied—but she was sure now what she'd heard. It was the voice from the night before.

"*Señora! Señora! Estas bien?* You okay, *Señora?*" Eduardo sounded panicky as he tried to locate his student.

Adrienne lay gasping in knee-deep water, adjusting her suit, her board still attached to her ankle by its cord. She sat up confused, unnerved and carnally alive. What the hell had just happened? A need she did not completely understand called her back to the sea. Everything in her told her to run from this, but she knew she could not. The temptation was too great. She had to go back.

"I'm okay," she answered boldly. "Let's try that again."

Eduardo lifted her board, turned it around, and after she climbed back up on it, he pulled her back out toward the place where they had begun. A new wave washed over them as they worked their way to deeper water.

You have the breasts of a goddess that react like those of a whore. You like pleasure, though you fight against it.

She shuddered, still raw and desirous from her last ride. So that had been foreplay. What would happen next? Smaller waves passed them, lapping against her skin like a warm tongue, teasing her and building her need. When they reached the place they had been before, Eduardo turned her board toward the beach.

"Eduardo?" she asked. "Do people ever say they hear—well, hear strange things out here?"

Eduardo laughed. "Maybe, *Señora*, perhaps you hear *Xocicolto*. The legend says when his time comes, he is here in these waters. But it is only an old story. I think you are not used to the sound of the waves."

Adrienne laughed. She felt so silly. Of course she was imagining it all. It was one thing to get older, but did she have to be crazy, too?

Eduardo buoyed himself at the back of her board with one arm and focused his gaze out into the beyond. Facing the beach, Adrienne could feel the smaller waves passing under her, teasing her with vibrating shudders from the board between her legs. She began to feel hot and dizzy, despite her contact with the cool water. Ringlets of currents continued to tease her between her toes. She lay down again, stretching her full frame against the board to rest and recover.

This made no sense. This was not who she was, yet the movement of the board and the coolness of the water licked at her pussy, tasting her juices, just as the voice had said it would. It worked up a passion in her she could not separate herself from. The pleasure was too intense and certainly too difficult to fight. She feared Eduardo turning his head and finding her thus, but there was no stopping now. In this position, the smaller waves washed over the back of her as well, continuing to move the board in its lusty fashion. Finding herself moved to an uncontrollable precipice, she felt a massive increase beneath her as water rushed more quickly past her head.

Don't fear me. I will set you free. Come with me. Come with me...

She felt Eduardo turn and prepare to push her.

"*Ahora, Señora,* NOW!"

As he pushed her toward land, the tumescence of the swell raised her higher than before. White water danced more passionately at her sides before pushing past her. She paddled as strongly as she could, taxing her wind and lightening her head.

On your knees... the voice demanded.

Adrienne, despite anything that had ever made sense to her, gave in and raised herself to her knees, gripping the front of the board to hold on. As the crest behind her rose, she felt a powerful undertow reorient her board, sending a surge of cold wash hard into her hot, aching cunt from behind. She felt the water between her legs, like a kind of forceful spout, fucking her from behind with a hard, cold member that plunged into her, giving her more pleasure than she had ever felt before. As the board shuddered up and down against the wake, she felt the sensation of the waterspout force in and out of her, throwing currents through her body. All the while, the wave roared its building passion in her ears.

The wave grew louder, and with each thrust she managed new angles to turn and adjust to stay abreast of the careening flow. This time both breasts were freed from her suit. Cold, wet hands seemed to grasp and pull at them as she felt the cold water dick drive deeper and deeper inside her. The sea boiled around her. Finally, unable to hold on to the feeling any longer, she let a guttural scream escape from way deep inside her, as she burst into a briny spray.

And then all was calm.

The voice whispered to her from under the surface. Her board floated gently over soft eddies, halting only when its rudder caught the sand below. She lay there, floating and pulling against the bottom, letting the sun splash over her and embrace her with a glow she could feel everywhere.

"*Señora*, maybe this is enough for today?" Eduardo asked when he finally reached her. His face showed worry that he had failed with this client. His concern brought her back to reality. What the hell had just happened, and what part had she had in it?

"Yes, that's enough for today, I think," she answered curtly. Eduardo showed her to the smaller casita the resort kept at this beach. A long, delicious dinner of fresh fish, tortillas and beer on the beach was the perfect ending to a perfect day. Between the surfing, her full stomach, and the time difference between Cabo and the East Coast, Adrienne was more than ready to retire to her bed and fall immediately to sleep.

She awoke to find a cool wetness wrapped around her. A sexy, salty smell she could actually taste filled her nose. She realized with a fright that she was not alone in her bed. She jumped up, gathering the bedding around her, covered her nakedness and shivered in fear. There was a man in the bed next to her, a very big man. He was naked and hard muscled; his long, wet black hair fell down his back. He moved slowly, turning to her.

"Why do you cover yourself? You are beautiful."

She tried to speak but was too frightened for any sound to escape her. He spoke again, looking into her eyes.

"Why do you show fear?"

Adrienne shook her head, despite an understanding growing inside her. He touched the sides of her face with cool hands, drawing one slowly down the side of her body.

"You know me. We are already lovers."

"*Xocicolto,*" she whispered with confusion as he slipped his hands under her and lifted her to him with no effort at all. She squeaked in mild protest as he pulled the covers away from her naked body. He smiled at her beauty, before pulling her closer to him and burying his head in her breast. This mythical man began to kiss her and whisper softly in an ancient tongue. She let him gently ravish her, afraid to move, but mostly because she was too tempted to resist.

"Why do you fear what your body does naturally? I saw you the first night, you know. You hide from your desire. You tie it up inside you. I knew if I could free you from this, you would become more than any woman I've had before. I have been here for hundreds of years, with many women, but I have not had anyone like you."

She shuddered with desire as he continued to explore her body. His tongue, his fingers, his lips found her, tasting her in places that she had never realized could be so alive. From time to time, he looked deeply into her eyes, as if asking how far she would let him go.

"It's only a dream, it's only a dream." She said it aloud to reassure herself. It was time to come back to reality, but did she want to? Did she really have to? His touching and probing rendered her incapable of anything other than seeking the pleasure in him that he was determined to find in her. His cool ocean fingers entered her hot places as they had in the sea, but in her bed they were more focused and real. He flicked her clit until she wanted to scream. Abruptly he stopped licking until his cold tongue found her nipples and his teeth bit them gently, coaxing them forward and making them hard. Soon, she was teeming, pulsing and set for detonation. He pulled away from her for a moment and, again, looked at her deeply, asking her questions and telling her things that needed no words. He was not old or young. He was, at once, timeless and of this time. As he was set away from her for the moment, she could read his rich, red skin. He ran his fingers through her thick, dark hair. She could see the life pulsing in his enormous manhood as he prepared her, pulled her close to him again, then entered her hot, wet cave that hungered for his every twitch and shudder. He moved in and out of her slowly at first, then, finding a rhythm between them, he quickened his thrusts. He reached a strong arm around each of her thighs and pulled her legs aside him, then lifting her up as he had on the sea, he drove into her, physically and metaphysically deeper than anyone—real or imagined—had before.

She felt herself rise higher and higher, his guttural utterances and her cries confirming their collective fervor. She felt something let go inside her. That thing that had been tied up within her was giving way. His earlier words echoed in her mind as she bucked wildly against him, no longer afraid of following and enjoying temptation. An unfamiliar wildness drove her as they tickled and tortured each other into a swollen, painful pleasure knot.

Outside, the wind rose with their jutting spasms, carrying first their groans, and finally their fiery screams across time. He ground his head into her chest to anchor himself against his passionate release, sending her into an uncontrollably pleasurable orgasmic fit.

Then they lay still, in the dark, for what seemed like an eternity. Neither dared speak, lest they break the spell.

Then he rose from their bed to stare out the window before turning to her, staring in her eyes long and hard. He then removed a leather rope that had been tied to his arm. He tied it tenderly around her arm and kissed her passionately.

"My time is short. I have only a few days, but I will come to you," he said softly and then faded away.

Adrienne woke with a start. She took inventory of the small casita, anchoring herself in reality before it all began to come back to her. *That was either one hell of a dream or I am losing my mind,* she thought. She cracked the door to peep outside. Along the beach, things were coming to life. Gathering locals limbered their bodies before heading out on their surfboards. Eduardo sat in the sand just outside her door with several travel cups that smelled, she noted gratefully, like coffee.

"*Señora*, you are awake early. Do you wish for some breakfast or do we have waves first?"

Adrienne giggled, then surprised herself with a full-on blush. It didn't matter anymore what was real and what was fantasy. All she knew was that she could not stop, and that if it was within her power, she would never let it end. Never had she felt more alive or sexual. Her midlife muck had turned into an out of this world midlife fuck!

"Waves," she answered, unequivocally. "Give me a minute to get dressed."

For two more glorious days, Adrienne road the waves like she'd been surfing her whole life. No longer needing Eduardo's help, she maneuvered her own board to great heights and through complex turns. She was convinced that *Xocicolto*'s strong hands held her safe, giving her the confidence to push herself more with each ride. Sometimes, she would surf all they way in, forcing the back of her board downward to stay atop the crest like a queen. But sometimes she still took the whole trip to shore on her knees or lying flat on her board.

And for two more nights, the Aztec prince came to her. They made love boldly, craving each other with zealous, overpowering emotion. He sought out all the secret places on her body that sent her soaring and pleading for him to fill her with his cold, salty essence. And when they could bear the prelude to their passion no longer, he drew her on top of him, skillfully maneuvering her up and down against his roiling crested member, just as he did with her each day in his watery form.

That third night, sensing that this could be their last, they pushed the limits of their beings. With a new and uncharacteristic boldness, Adrienne tickled and teased the places within him, draining him of his godliness and in her bed, turning this Mexican royalty into a mere mortal. As her bravado blossomed,

Xociolto relinquished control, allowing an exquisite, mutual exchange of reawakening pleasures. She saturated him with her warmth, as he cooled her with his deep sea touch.

She laid him back, never removing her eyes from his. Then, taking his member gently in her hands, she leaned down to lick the length of him. She could feel a pulsing begin deep inside the emerging organ. She inhaled his cold, salty scent, following the quivering veins back down to their base with her tongue and nibbled at the fruit there. He began to whisper the ancient words, raising a heat in her that she had come to expect. He sensed the connection, and his speech became broken. He raised himself from her and looked into her soul. He knew she was changed. He knew she was his. He knew he was hers. Rolling over onto her back as he pushed into her, Adrienne raised her legs high above her head, sending them thrashing with abandon into a shared rapture.

But once they were still, she could tell something was different with him. His skin felt warm and dry. Unable to speak, barely able to breathe, they lay twisted together. Finally, he turned to her and kissed the place where he'd tied the cord to her arm. He removed it, held it in his hand, then pushed her arm up above her head, kissing her gently up the inside of her arm. When he reached her face, he gazed at her with a drained sadness that made her start to cry. He licked the tears from her face that were soon mingled with tears of his own.

"I am weak at the end of my time. I am called back to the place where I must go."

With that, he produced an oddly shaped golden bead.

"This is something that was once precious to me. It held great value to my people. It is as old as I am. Perhaps older than you can comprehend. If you will wear it, it will connect you to me for all time."

He threaded the bead onto the leather cord, and this time, tied it around Adrienne's neck. He tried to sit up but faltered. She sat up in their bed to hold him, leaning him back slowly against her, cradling him in her arms.

"Stay with me," she pleaded, knowing before he spoke what his answer had to be.

He smiled softly at her, raised a weak arm and began to gently caress her cheek.

"I must return to the place where I belong or I will be no more."

A golden light appeared from the heavens, illuminating a path into the sea. *Xocicolto* left her and walked into it, seemingly gaining strength once the sea closed in around him. He looked up into the light, stretched his arms out wide and cast a loving glance back at Adrienne. Then he and the light were gone.

Eduardo knocked on her trailer door, as he had done two mornings hence.

"*Señora*, we surf?" he asked.

"No, Eduardo. Today we go home."

On the way back to the resort, Adrienne kept one hand at the hollow of her neck, touching the beautiful bead her lover had placed there. Returned to her casita, she packed her things and prepared for tomorrow's flight home. She sat alone that night on her private balcony, staring out to sea. She marveled at her experience over the last few days. Opening her heart had opened her senses. She no longer felt old and bored with life as she had on her arrival. She was leaving with a new lease on life, a new sense of curiosity, adventure, and lustfulness. Adrienne wept softly through her smiles, as heard the surf sing its message of *Come to me. Come to me...*

A blissful knowing pull drew her to walk down to the beach.

Unlike the day of her arrival, the sea in front of her resort was as smooth as glass. The jutting rocks stood out as silent sentinels, basking in waves that slowly rippled around them. She walked toward the sea, allowing the surf to wash over her toes. Feeling a strange vibration at her neck, Adrienne reached for the bead, momentarily afraid of the power pulsating around her neck. She panicked and clutched at the cord.

You are mine. You will always be mine. The sound of his whisper enveloped and calmed her, and forever awoke a sensuous awareness within her.

The bead around her neck began to glow. Its vibration intensified and ripples of pleasure reverberated throughout her body. She could feel his breath not cold this time, but hot against her neck.

You will always be in me. I will always be in you.

"You will always be in me. I will always be in you," she repeated into the wind.

Then, as the bead began to darken and cool, she knew he was gone.

The next morning, with only a couple of hours to make her plane, Adrienne rushed about the casita throwing everything of hers into anything she could carry as Eduardo waited by her door.

"*Señora*, it is the time that we must go to the *aeropuerto*."

She smiled at him and handed him the heaviest bag. Before following him, she turned and took one last look toward the magical Sea of Cortez. Adrienne felt a small tingle at her neck, and somewhere else, deeper inside.

"Eduardo?" she finally asked, feeling a million miles away. "The sea is very different here from the way it was when I first arrived, isn't it?"

"*Sí, Señora*. It was *Xocicolto*. But he is gone now. I told you, it is a special time. He comes only *una vez* every year."

"Yes, Eduardo. Every year. And you know what? From now on, so will I!"

TRANSLATION SENSATION

Sasha James

The hardest thing about writing erotica is crossing the (sexual) line with style and class.

—Sasha James

*E*n *Français*

"*N'arrête pas, n' arrête pas,*" Genevieve kept repeating over and over. By the confused look on her American lover's face, she could tell that he had no idea that she was asking for "more please." He had stopped kissing her neck, and she wanted desperately for him to continue. She started pointing to the spot that his lips had just vacated, hoping that he would pick up the hint.

"Oh, you want some more?" Mark said, and picked up where he had left off.

His kisses began trailing from her thin neck to her cleavage. He unbuttoned the tiny pearl buttons on her red silk blouse until her lace bra was exposed. Mark hesitated long enough to admire her sexy underwear. Her bra was thin enough for him to see the rosy color of her nipples. "Damn, you French chicks really have the feminine thing down to a science."

"*Pardon?*" she asked, wrinkling her nose. Now it was Genevieve who didn't understand.

Mark listened to her French words, which floated in the air like a sweet symphony. He didn't know what she was saying but knew they weren't the same words as before. They didn't understand each other's language, but that didn't really matter. What mattered was that they spoke the same body language, and right now her body was speaking volumes. The way she was poking out her breasts and moving closer to him on the sofa was telling him to proceed, and proceed he did.

Mark unsnapped her bra, causing her tits to spill out. Unlike most women he had been with, she was au natural, no implants, all flesh. He placed his hand underneath her right boob and jiggled it just to make sure. "Yep, all woman," he mused, as her titty shook like Jell-O.

Genevieve reached for the back of his head and guided him toward her waiting nipple. Realizing that words were useless, she decided to utilize hand gestures, and pinched her nipple with her thumb and index finger.

Marked took her clue and began to suckle her tit like he was trying to extract milk.

Genevieve threw her head back on the sofa cushions and enjoyed the succulent sensation. She couldn't believe that only a few hours ago, she had stepped off the plane at Kennedy Airport, and now she was in the midst of a heated sexual experience.

The flight from Charles de Gaulle to Kennedy airport was long, and Genevieve should have slept the entire way, but she was too excited to close her eyes. She had dreamt of coming to America, especially New York, since she was a child. Seeing postcards and pictures from friends and relatives who had been abroad had piqued her interest at an early age, and she often daydreamed about seeing the Statue of Liberty, the Golden Gate Bridge and other famous American monuments.

Now that she was an adult, her dream was finally coming to fruition. Genevieve had joined an Internet social network, and had met some really cool Americans, who persuaded her to come to the States. Their urging, coupled with her long-seated desire, was all she needed to finally make the trip.

Genevieve owned a small *boulangerie-pâtisserie* in the sixteenth *arrondissement* with her fiancé. Their bakery was in an affluent part of Paris and was extremely successful, allowing her to splurge on a ten-day holiday in the States. Jean-Paul, her fiancé, stayed behind to mind the shop, allowing her to fulfill her childhood dream before they settled down and had a family.

Her first stop was Manhattan, and then on to Chicago and California before heading back home. Having lived in France all of her life, Genevieve's English was poor at best. Even though she learned the foreign language in grade school, she hadn't had much use for it, until now. She had brushed up on a few key phrases before coming to the States, like, "Hello, my name is...," "Please," "Excuse me," and "Thank you." And she hoped to pick up more English while she was in New York.

The customs line was long but moved swiftly and soon Genevieve had her passport stamped and was free to enter the United States. She traded her Euros for dollars at the currency exchange and then headed to baggage claim. After she retrieved her luggage, she headed outside to the taxi line.

"Where ya goin'?" asked the taxi driver in a thick Brooklyn accent, once she climbed in the backseat.

Genevieve took out the brochure for the hotel and handed it to him.

"Twenty-fourth and Seventh, coming right up."

Genevieve was so excited that she perched herself on the edge of the seat and peered out of the window. She watched in awe as the streets of New York whizzed by. The afternoon sun was shining bright, and sunlight bounced off the tops of skyscrapers. The city's bridges—especially the Brooklyn Bridge—were also a wonder to her, standing tall and strong over the East River.

Soon, they were pulling up in front of the hotel, located in Chelsea. She paid the driver and got out.

Once she had checked into her room she hooked up her laptop, wanting to let her friend know that she had made it safely to the hotel. Genevieve logged on to her email account, and sure enough there was an email from her American friend, Barbara. She clicked on the email, copied the text and then pasted it onto a translation website, which interpreted it into French.

Hey there, hope you had a good flight. I'm working this afternoon, but can meet you later this evening to show you a really good time.

Genevieve typed her response back in French and used the same copy and paste method to translate her words to English.

Sounds good. I can't wait. She and Barb had been email buddies for the past few months, and she couldn't wait to meet in person.

After sending Barb the hotel information, Genevieve logged off, took a brief power nap, and then, before heading out to explore the city, she stopped at the front desk and dropped off an envelope. Some of her New York Internet buddies had suggested that she check out the Village and other cool places in the city. She followed their instructions, took her time and browsed in and out of shops and boutiques along Seventh Avenue. New

York was similar to Paris in that there were people everywhere, and everyone seemed to be in a hurry. She looked at the buildings and noted that most of the architecture was old, though of course not as old as that in France. But some structures had ornate masonry work that she found interesting. Although she was a stranger to the city and didn't speak much English, she didn't feel like an alien; she felt right at home.

Before long, Genevieve found her way to the West Village and into Bar Pitti, a trendy Italian restaurant, with an awesome outdoor café, perfect for people-watching. Celebrities were known to frequent the place, as well as a smattering of the beautiful people.

"*Buona sera, bella*," the handsome Italian host greeted her.

Genevieve smiled broadly. She may not have known much English, but she knew Italian well. She returned the greeting, and they stood there and conversed in Italian for a few moments. He flirted shamelessly, complimenting her on her beauty before seating her at a choice outdoor table.

The waiter promptly came over, and she ordered a glass of wine. When he came back with her drink, he rattled off a list of specials in English and told her to take her time. Genevieve didn't understand, so she just smiled and nodded her head as he spoke.

Genevieve glanced over the menu. It was all in English so she ordered what she knew, spaghetti Bolognese, and sipped her wine as she glanced around the restaurant.

She looked to her left and instantly locked eyes with a handsome stranger. He was staring intently at her, and his gaze was mesmerizing. Even from across the café, she could see his smoldering brown eyes. He had chocolate brown skin, a clean-shaven head, a chiseled jawline, full lips and a keen nose. He wore a white shirt, underneath a navy blue suit. Even wearing a suit,

Genevieve could see that he had broad shoulders. He was alone, sitting comfortably with his arm draped across the back of the chair and his legs crossed. He was swirling red wine around in his glass. He had an air of confidence about him that Genevieve found sexy.

He tilted his glass in her direction and nodded his head, acknowledging her presence.

Genevieve blushed shyly, then slowly licked her lips suggestively. She was an engaged woman and had no right admiring, let alone flirting with another man, but she couldn't help herself. She had never dated a black man before and found herself wondering what it would be like to kiss his luscious lips. Would they engulf her mouth? Would they feel soft against hers? Would they...

Arrête! she thought, telling herself to stop. Genevieve diverted her eyes away from his. Hailing from France, the country of love, she was extremely sensual. However, she had no business lusting after another man. She looked down at the diamond engagement ring on her left hand, and it was sparkling up at her as a reminder that she was spoken for.

"Excuse me. Do you mind if I join you?"

Genevieve looked up, startled. She had been staring down at her ring and didn't see the stranger cross the patio. Now he was standing directly in front of her table talking to her. She could make out a few of his words, but the rest were foreign to her. "*Pardon?*" she replied in her heavy French accent.

I should have known she was European. She's too exotic looking to be American, he thought. Mark took in Genevieve's essence. She had smooth alabaster skin and thick black hair that she wore parted down the center, cascading over her shoulders and down her back. Her lips were thin, but the red lipstick she wore made them look luscious and inviting. She wore a snug, crimson blouse, the exact color of her lipstick, and a black skirt that rose above her knees as she sat, cross-legged. She oozed sex appeal but not in a vulgar way. She seemed comfortable in her skin and was not trying to be provocative. Mark could feel heat beginning to rise from within. This woman, whoever she was, was turning him on, and she hadn't even uttered a complete sentence. There seemed to be a hedonistic connection between them. He sensed it from across the room, and now that he was standing close, there was no denying their chemistry. If they were wild animals in the jungle, he would be mounting her by now and fucking her brains out. And just like animals, they had sniffed out each other's attraction. But unlike beasts in the wild kingdom, he had to act with decorum.

"Do you speak English?" he asked, slowly.

Genevieve put up her index finger and thumb, put them close together, and said, "*Un peu.*"

He pulled out the chair across from her. "Well, a little is better than none. Do you mind?" he asked before sitting down.

Genevieve didn't know what he said but figured he was asking to sit down. She nodded her head yes, and then said, "*Puis-je m'asseoir sur votre visage, pendant que vous mangez, ma chatte?*"

"I don't know what you just say, but it sure sounds good."

Mark had no idea that she had asked to sit on his face while he ate her pussy.

Genevieve smiled slyly at her brazen words. Saying whatever she wanted was a major turn-on. Being able to voice her inner thoughts was liberating. This was Genevieve's last vacation as a single woman, and it seemed a waste not to take full advantage of her freedom.

"Hi, my name is Mark." He smiled and extended his hand.

She shook his hand. "Genevieve."

Mark held her hand for a moment. Her skin was as soft as a baby's. He reluctantly released her hand and placed it gently back on the table.

"Would you like to move your seating, sir?" the waiter asked, noticing that Mark had migrated to another table.

"Yes, please." Mark noticed that Genevieve was also drinking red wine and decided to order a bottle. "Also, can you bring us a bottle of cabernet, and an assortment of appetizers? Did she order her dinner yet?"

"Yes, sir."

"Well, in that case, I'll have the fish of the day," he informed the waiter.

"Sure thing."

Genevieve listened to their exchange, understanding little but not caring. Her full attention was drawn to the handsome black American. As Mark was talking to the waiter, she stole a few glances at him. He was even more attractive up close. When he spoke, deep dimples pierced his chiseled cheeks. His teeth were so bright and perfect that they seemed artificial. His voice was deep and resonating. He was confident and commanded attention. Even though Genevieve had only been in his presence for mere moments, she was smitten. She had met black men in France, but none were as suave and debonair as this guy. He was as smooth as silk, and she sat back and watched him work.

After the waiter had gone, Mark scooted closer to the table. "I hope you're hungry," he said, very slowly. He noticed that she had a blank expression on her face, so he picked up the fork on the table and lifted it to his mouth.

From his gesture, Genevieve guessed that he was talking about eating. "*Oui, oui,*" she said, shaking her head yes, though her appetite was less for food and more for this delicious man.

"Here's your wine, sir," the waiter said, presenting the bottle to Mark.

Mark looked at the label, made sure it was what he had ordered, and then nodded his head. The waiter poured him a sip to taste. After Mark approved, the waiter poured them each a glass of the ruby colored liquid.

Mark started to ask Genevieve how long she was going to be in town, but he knew that she wouldn't understand him, so he just clinked his glass to hers and said, "Cheers."

"*A votre santé,*" she toasted, wishing him good health.

They drank in silence for a while, until the waiter brought out a dazzling array of food, everything from calamari to antipasto.

Mark was surprised to see that Genevieve wasn't shy. She prepared his plate first and then her own. She didn't pick at her food like some of his dates; instead she enjoyed the delicious appetizers. *Good, she has a healthy appetite. I wonder if her sexual appetite is as strong,* he found himself thinking.

Genevieve noticed that he wasn't eating. She then made the same gesture with her fork that he had made, indicating that he should eat.

Mark took her cue and began munching. Her beauty had taken away his appetite. The only thing he was hungry for at the moment was a taste of her pussy. He had been in Bar Pitti many times, but never had a woman commanded his attention like Genevieve. It must have been a combination of her beauty and her sexuality, and also the fact that he had spent the last three days upstate at a male mentoring retreat. The weekend had been great, with fatherless boys from the inner city meeting and bonding with successful men. Mark was a community organizer and had spearheaded the retreat. He had enjoyed every moment but was now ready for some female company, and Ms. Sexy Frenchwoman fit the bill perfectly.

When they finished their dinner, the waiter came, cleared their plates and returned to refill their glasses.

Genevieve stole glances at Mark as they sipped their wine. She was curious to know more about him, but the language barrier was in the way. The few English words she knew were whirling around in her head as she tried to formulate a sentence. *"Vous avez apprécié le repas,* meal?"

Mark knitted his brow. He didn't quite understand what she was saying. "Excuse me?"

The forks were gone from the table, so she put her hand to her mouth as if she were eating while smiling broadly and letting the sound "Mmm," slip through her lips.

"Oh, yes, I enjoyed dinner!"

Genevieve smiled, knowing that she had gotten her point across. She clicked her glass with his in a toasting gesture. The evening air was warm, and the company of an attractive man, coupled with the wine, was making her feel tingly inside. She wanted him badly. She had heard stories of black men having enormous dicks and wanted to find out for herself if that was true. She decided to seize the opportunity. And why not? She was on foreign soil and what she did in the States would stay safely in the States.

Mark returned her smile. She seemed to be at ease with him, and he was thrilled. He wasn't the player type, but when he saw someone he wanted, he wasted no time going after her, and he wanted this French woman badly.

"Tu es très beau. Je vais te baiser," she told him smiling.

"Uh-huh," he replied, having no clue what she was saying but mesmerized by the singsong quality of her voice.

Genevieve laughed, amused and aroused that she'd just told a stranger that she found him handsome and wanted to fuck him.

"Yes to whatever you just said," Mark said, smiling back.

When the bottle was finished, Mark motioned for the waiter and gave him his credit card. Once the bill was paid, he got up and helped Genevieve with her chair. There was a jazz joint around the corner, and he thought he'd take her there.

"Do you like jazz?" he asked.

"Jazz? No," she answered. *"Mais j'aime une grosse bite."* Genevieve bit her lip mischievously, wondering if Mark had any idea that she'd just told him that she didn't like jazz, but she liked a big dick.

"Oh," he said, sounding disappointed about the jazz and not sure what else she was saying, but if it meant spending time together, he and his cock were game.

Genevieve walked slightly ahead of Mark. She wanted to go back to her hotel. She wasn't interested in listening to jazz or having drinks. She had something much more exciting in mind. She was meeting Barb later and thought that the three of them could experience New York together.

Mark sensed that she wanted to go elsewhere, so he let her lead the way. Once again the language barrier prevented them from communicating their exact thoughts. They passed several bars and lounges along with way. *Obviously, she doesn't want to stop for a drink,* he thought.

Genevieve knew that she was being bold, but being in New York and feeling the electric energy of the city was making her even bolder than normal. Definitely not the wallflower, shy type, Genevieve lived in the moment, and the moment was telling her to follow her thirst and obey her lust. She continued walking, until she came to her hotel. She walked through the doors without looking behind, hoping that Mark was following her every step.

Now that's what I'm talking about, he thought to himself, as they stepped into the elevator. *This night is getting better and better.*

When the elevator reached the tenth floor, Genevieve stepped out, made a left and walked down the hall. She stopped at her room, put the keycard in the slot and opened the door.

As soon as the door shut, Genevieve grabbed him to her. "*Embrasse-moi*," she said, translating her words with her mouth. The Frenchwoman began French kissing the black American man, her tongue doing a duet with his. With Genevieve in his arms, he began moving toward the bed.

When they reached the king-size bed, she pushed his chest lightly, indicating that she wanted him to lie down. She then climbed on top and straddled him. His thick lips tasted delicious, and she wanted more.

Mark loved her aggressiveness and didn't waste any time unbuttoning her blouse and tasting her ample breasts. "Damn, baby, you got some pretty titties," he said, admiring her breasts.

"*Embrasse-moi les nichons*," she said, rubbing her boobs and making kissing sounds with her lips.

"My pleasure!" he said, beginning to pick up a little French. *Embrasse-moi* apparently meant "kiss me." Mark buried his head in between her cleavage, kissing one tit and then the other.

"Ohhh," she said, and began spouting off a string of French words, telling him to suck her tit. "*Suce mon sein.*"

As Mark was feasting on her rack, he felt someone touch his bald head. He looked up at Genevieve thinking that she was rubbing his globe. "What the..." his words caught in his throat.

"I'm Barb. She left a key for me at the front desk," explained the beautiful blonde woman. "*Bonsoir, Genevieve. Et si on faisait ménage à trois.*"

"A threesome! Hell yes! The more the merrier!" Mark said. Finally some French he understood.

"Good," Barb said, looking Mark up and down.

Not detecting an accent, he asked. "You're not from France, too, are you?"

She continued rubbing his head, and at the same time began pinching Genevieve's nipples that had been left unattended. "No, we met over the Internet. I speak a little French, and with the free translation dictionary online, we are able to communicate. We're both curious about alternative relationships, so when she told me she was coming to New York," Barb leaned down and kissed Genevieve on the mouth, "I offered to be her tour guide."

Mark was getting hotter and harder by the moment. He couldn't believe that he had stumbled into a fucking *Penthouse* fantasy.

"Take off that dress; you have on too many clothes," he told Barb.

She stood up, unzipped her slinky black dress and let it fall to the floor. "You like what you see?"

Mark's jaw nearly dropped as he stared at her naked body. Her boobs were even bigger than Genevieve's. "What are you, a 38D?" he asked.

"No, sweetie, I'm a 40EE." She put her hands underneath each breast, and jiggled them. "And they're all mine!"

"My dick is so hard right now," he said, unbuckling his belt.

"I hope it stays hard all night."

"Don't worry about that." Mark got up and completely disrobed, as did Genevieve.

"Damn, I don't know who to fuck first," he said, looking from one to the other.

Genevieve couldn't keep her eyes off of his dick. It was twice as long as her fiancé's and three times as thick. The myth was right, and she couldn't wait to taste him. "*Je peux te sucer?*" she said, asking to suck him.

Mark began stroking his shaft. "You want this big dick, Ms. Frenchy?"

"*Oui. J' adore une grosse bite,*" she said again, eased over to him, and began sucking his cock.

"She likes your big dick," Barb translated. "That makes two of us."

While Genevieve was enjoying his chocolate stick, Barb got up, went across the room, picked up a black leather bag and brought it back to the bed.

"What's that?" he said, in between breaths.

Barb reached inside and took out a mini vibrator. "This is a clit stimulator." She handed it to him and then lay down with her legs spread wide open.

Mark didn't ask any more questions. He turned on the tiny device, found Barb's clit and began teasing it, as Genevieve continued teasing the head of his dick.

"Yeah, baby, that's it. That's it!" Barb moaned, already on the verge of cumming.

"Damn, this shit is hot!" he said, looking down at one woman blowing him, while he clit-fucked another. "Okay, baby, that's good," he said, running his hands through Genevieve's raven black hair. He didn't want to cum so fast, and with the way she was loving on his dick, it wouldn't be too long before he squirted his load. He turned off the vibrator.

"Why'd you stop?" Barb asked.

"Because I want Genevieve to show you some of her skills. I think she can do a better job than this thing," he said, tossing the pocket rocket to the floor.

"Hmm, I like the sound of that," Barb said, reaching for the other woman. "*Bouffe ma chatte.*"

Genevieve's eyes lit up as she smiled and licked her lips. She climbed on top of Barb and wasted no time sucking her huge nipples. She then trailed her tongue down Barb's chest to her hairy triangle, parted her pussy lips and began feasting on her engorged clit.

Barb grabbed Genevieve's hair, pushing her face farther into her canal.

"Oh, shit, this is so fucking wicked!" Mark exclaimed. Watching the two women make love was better than any porno flick he had ever seen. His dick was now harder than Chinese arithmetic, and he was ready to fuck! He eased up behind Genevieve while she had Barb's head. He rubbed her soft ass, and then put his hand underneath until he found her wet box. He parted her buttcheeks and entered her pussy from behind.

Genevieve felt him behind her and stuck her ass out farther so that he could have easier access.

At first he had a hard time trying to penetrate her tight hole, but as soon as the head entered, he slipped inside her with ease and began fucking her slowly, taking his time, enjoying every second.

"*Plus fort. Fort!*" Genevieve demanded, thrusting harder to make him understand.

"Shit, baby, if harder is what you want, harder is what you'll get."

The three of them were now interconnected, with Mark pounding Genevieve's pussy and Genevieve giving Barb a clit special. The only sounds heard were an Anglo-French mix of erotic ecstasy.

"Don't shoot your wad, baby. Save some for me," Barb requested.

Mark pulled out before he came and then said, "Switch positions."

Barb quickly got up and traded places with Genevieve. She too wanted some of his beef. "I want you to butt-fuck me," she told him, and then reached into her bag. She took out a tube of lubricant, unscrewed the top and smeared the clear gel on her asshole. After she was finished, Mark took the tube from her and coated his dick with the gooey gel.

"This night keeps getting better and better," he mused, as he entered Barb's ass.

"Oh, shit, that hurts so goood!" she screamed out.

Mark fucked her like a man possessed. It wasn't often that a woman requested a good butt fuck, and tonight, he planned on giving her exactly what she wanted. The fucking was so good that he couldn't help but cum in her warm ass.

"That was awesome!" Barb then turned to Genevieve. "I'm sorry, babe, for neglecting you," she told her in French, "but that chocolate dick was just too good to ignore. Come here and let me make it up to you." Barb reached into her bag of tricks again, took out a large black dildo, lubed it up, and rammed it into Genevieve's hot box. Since Mark's equipment was temporarily deflated, she took over and began fucking her like a wild woman.

"Oh, *oui, oui*," Genevieve sang out.

Mark watched them go at it and began stroking his dick, trying to resurrect his soldier. He wanted to get back in the game but for now was getting off watching them.

"Is it good to you, baby?" Barb asked, working the vibrator in and out.

"*N'arrête pas*," Genevieve replied: "Don't stop."

Barb continued until Genevieve's face twisted in a painfully pleasant expression, indicating that she was cumming hard.

"My turn," Barb said, wanting some of the ever-ready vibrator.

Genevieve slipped her fingers into Barb's pussy, making sure it was wet before ramming her with the dildo.

"Fuck me, bitch!" Barb yelled out.

"*Prends-lae salope*," she replied, saying "Take this slut."

Genevieve kept working the wand until Barb screamed out. "Oh, shit, I'm cumming. I'm cumming!"

Mark's eyes were glued to them, as he jacked off. He felt his cream rising to the top, so he got up and stood over the women. As soon as Barb reached the pinnacle, he sprayed them with a stream of hot juicy cum, and then collapsed onto the bed.

Their heated sexcapade had worn them out, and they fell into a deep sleep. Genevieve awoke in the middle of the night and glanced over at her lovers, who were still sound asleep. Her vacation had gotten off to a grand start, and if nothing else exciting happened while she was in the States, that would be okay. She had experienced fucking a black man, and a woman; now she was ready to go back to Paris, get married and start a family.

It was unclear what had possessed her to act with such wild sexual abandon, but she had no regrets. With a satisfied smile on her face, she shrugged her shoulders and thought, *Je n'y peux rien, je suis comme ca.* "Can't help the way that I feel."

LEAD ME INTO TEMPTATION…

Introduction by Lori Bryant-Woolridge

Temptation is the fuel for a fully expressed life.
—Lori Bryant-Woodridge

N ow that you and your imagination are revved up and ready to purr, allow yourself to be *led into temptation* with the following tasty, to-be-continued story bites designed to get your creative (and other) juices flowing. Make this erotic tome uniquely personal by picking your favorite sexy starter (or choose all three) and finishing your own sultry tale on the blank pages that follow. Don't feel the need to complete these stories on your own. By all means, grab your favorite lover and spend the night researching and then writing your personal erotic tale together. Turn this exercise into a special date night. Light some candles, uncork a bottle of your favorite wine and grab a pen. Take turns reading the stories and suggesting what scenes should come next. Before you know it, you'll have written a story of your own and fired up a lot more than your imaginations! As a sensuality coach, I often give this exercise to my clients as an exercise to help free their sensual muse and build intimacy and sexual communication with their partners. My single clients find it to be a real confidence booster as well. I think you will too.

Explore the fantasies lurking in your head, and find out for yourself how much fun and how liberating it is to write about things that go bump and grind in the night!

LEAD ME INTO TEMPTATION...

SHAVED BY THE BELLE

"SHIT. FUCK. SHIT. FUCK. SHIT. FUCK. DAMN!"

The stream of curse words that come tumbling out of my mouth seem wholly appropriate for the disastrous situation I currently find myself in. I have a little over an hour before my husband gets home for his surprise anniversary celebration. But instead of finding the smooth, shaved pussy of a wanton wife awaiting him, he is going to find my tortured tinklebelle that now looks like it has been deforested by a circus chimp armed with a fucking weed whacker.

My DIY job went terribly wrong and now I'm standing here sporting a gruesome patchwork of pubes. Sad and unsightly? Hell, yes. Smooth and sexy? Not so fucking much. Now what? It is too late to get an appointment, and I have no idea who or where to call anyway. There's only one thing left to do: call in the cavalry.

"Please be home. Please be home," I pray aloud as Tamara's phone continues to ring. After six rings, she finally picks up, sounding either sleepy, high or freshly fucked.

"I need help," I announce. The panic in my voice must have cut through her yet-to-be-determined fog because she perks right up.

"Are you okay? What's wrong? Should I call nine-one-one?"

"Just get over here, NOW!" I hang up the phone and immediately burst into tears. I really want my romantic dinner and sexy unveiling to be perfect, but things are off to a bad start.

Tam lives about fifteen minutes away, and while I wait for her, I decide to set the table and put the pork tenderloin, Brooks's favorite, into the oven. By the time I have it all prepped and am sliding it into the oven, I hear Tamara's frantic knock on my door.

"Girl, what's happened?" she cries out as soon as she is inside.

"You have to fix it!" I say, as I fling my black silk robe open to reveal my clumsy handiwork.

Tam bursts out laughing. She just stands there chortling and damn near choking at my expense. "What the fuck...ha...ha... have you done to your damn self?"

"Just shut up and come fix it," I demand, grabbing her hand and pulling her back into the bedroom.

"Fine, but you owe me. I'd planned on staying in all night and fucking myself silly. I scored some of the best clit weed I've had in a long-ass time." Clit weed is Tamara's term for marijuana that goes straight to her clitoris, making it fat, hard and way, way orgasmic. She isn't a pothead by any means—that is until it comes to clit weed. Then she's a fucking junkie.

"Whatever. But you have to do it quick. Brooks will be home in less than an hour."

"Okay, let me take a good look." I pulled my robe open

again, allowing her to peruse the situation. "Only thing you can do now is shave the damn thing bald."

"What the fuck do you think I was trying to do?"

"Calm down. I need a razor, shaving cream, a bowl of warm water, a towel and a match."

"A MATCH? What the hell do you need a match for?" I ask, while visions of bushfires blaze through my head.

"To light my joint so you can take a hit, calm the fuck down, and let me do what I need to do so I can get back to what I want to do."

"I don't need a joint to relax."

"I'm about to put a sharp razor all in and around your pussy lips. You're already aggravated and in a hurry. Need I go on? Just take a hit and let's do this. Time is a-tickin' and you want to be ready for your anniversary lickin'."

"Tee-hee," I say sarcastically as I speed off to get the re-quested items. I return and take a couple of tokes before passing it to Tam. She declines, declaring she's already had enough, and instead pops in her mouth some "curiously strong" spearmint Altoid gum.

"You're not too high, are you? I'm not trying to replace my pubic hair with Band-Aids."

"Shush and let me concentrate. This shouldn't take long to clean up."

I do as I am told and lie back on my bed, naked under my open robe, with my knees up and resting together. Suddenly it dawns on me—even for the best of friends, this is a truly up-close-and-personal situation, and for that reason, and all the others she espoused, I am happy Tamara brought that joint.

"Open," she says, gently prying my knees apart and apply-ing shaving cream to my crotch. She works the cool froth into my pubic area and begins to pull the razor across the top of my mound and down the lips of my pussy. I close my eyes as I feel and hear the gentle scraping of wiry hair remnants being removed. Tam herself makes no sound as she works quickly and gently. I listen as she swishes the razor through the bowl of water and taps it against the edges. Tamara returns her hands to between my legs and pushes my knees closer to the mattress, scraping the hair away. Again I hear *swish, swish, tap, tap* and then once again feel her hands moving back in. Only this time, I feel cool metal against my sensitive pussy lips. The clit weed is really kicking in because I feel deliciously vulnerable splayed wide open as she runs the razor up my tender, naked skin. My pussy is actually tingling and I am loving the sensation. My clit hiccups as my nipples harden in response.

Tamara gently separates my labia and shaves away the remaining stubble. A moan has been sent by my brain but my mouth refuses to release it. My breasts and clit are screaming in tandem for attention. This shit feels sexy and slutty and fabulous as hell! I am definitely aroused and I force my eyes to stay shut, afraid that any movement will give me away. "Almost done," Tamara whispers. A waft of peppermint reaches my nose and adds to the sensory delight. "I'll be right back."

I have no idea where she is going but take the opportunity to slide my hand down past my thigh. The skin of my hand comes into contact with pudding soft folds of flesh. My tinklebelle is as smooth and soft as, yes, a baby's behind. The sensation is amazing and immediately I am craving the touch of tongue on my bare belle. As my left hand gives each nipple a quick pinch and a roll, I start to move my right hand toward my dying-to-be-sucked clit but stop when I hear Tamara's footsteps approaching. She says nothing but I hear the sound of friction made by two hands being quickly rubbed together. Within seconds I feel a warm slickness being spread around my aching pussy. I smell roses and know immediately that she has found my body oil and is rubbing—no massaging—my hairless twat. I feel every rub and gentle tug like I've never experienced them before. My vagina is much more sensitive without the jungle. Why had I taken so long to do this?

Some of the oil has dripped down into the crack of my ass and as I am enjoying the slippery sensation along with my pussy massage, I hear a gentle buzz fill the room. The pleasure of this marijuana-enhanced sensation is too tempting and I am still unwilling to open my eyes to investigate. I feel the lips of my pussy being gently tugged open and feel a wet, gooey mass seduce my clit with a perfectly modulated vibration. Within seconds, I feel a cool, peppermint thrill spread up and down the thin walls of my vagina. Tam circles my engorged bud with the vibrator and I can feel my juicy wetness drip down my hairless valley and pool beneath me.

I hear a moan and the sound of Tamara gulping back her arousal. She too is turned on by all of this and I decide if I just don't open my eyes, this can remain a true fantasy and neither of us will have to deal with the embarrassment of this delicious, unintended seduction.

The hurts-so-good burning sensation is intensified when Tam leans over and blows her peppermint breath directly on my clitoris. Immediately, it begins to throb and she responds by firing it up with intermittent waves of battery-operated bliss. I feel a gummy concentration of cool at the tip of my nib, still not knowing what it is and frankly not giving a damn because I am so close to spraying pussy juice right in front of my best friend that it's not funny.

I want to let go so badly, but I am embarrassed.

"It's okay. Let it go," she says reading my humiliation and granting me permission to detonate. She ups the vibration a notch and within seconds I am coming in waves and waves of pleasure. My hands automatically cup my breasts, pulling at my nipples, which intensifies my orgasm. Tamara continues to rub my bare and swollen pussy, watching in fascination as it twitches and pops.

I relax into the fading tide and open my eyes in time to see two things: Tamara pulling her wad of gum from my pussy and sticking it back into her mouth, and Brooks walking through the bedroom door.

Please do continue...

LEAD ME INTO TEMPTATION...

TAKE A MEETING

You pause on the sidewalk in front of his building. You've never done anything like this before. But then again, you've never met anyone like *him* before. Whoever first uttered the cliché, "took my breath away," had obviously spent time in the presence of this magnificent specimen of a man.

It isn't that his looks are particularly outstanding. Oh, he is damn fine all right, but not in the meet-my-stylist, Hollywood way that most girls swoon over. He is masculinity personified, with a combination of divergent qualities that make him so very tempting: tough but awkwardly tender; intellectual, yet street savvy; sophisticated, yet down with the cause.

He has the timeless physique of an athlete whose ego still gives a damn—tall and lean with runner's legs. His perfect head is bald, with a slight sheen that beckons to be kissed; his skin is the color of dark chocolate pudding and just as soft and creamy to the touch. His sable, brown eyes are magnetic. They have a piercing quality about them, not hard or intimidating, just a haunting and unforgettable pull to them. But the true lure is his smile. This man has a slightly gapped grin that lights a fire in his warm, sexy eyes and pulls at the corners of his mouth before erupting into a happy homicide kind of smile. We're talking killer, drop-you-to-the-floor deadly.

You hadn't realized just how lethal until he flashed it at you one evening at a party. You'd seen him at other events around town because as big as Manhattan is, the African American social circle is pretty intimate. You'd never exchanged more than a few polite words, but the few you did—though nothing very special—were transported on communication lines powered by sensual electricity. Every "hello" was foreplay. Every "nice to see you" was tantamount to a kiss. And every damn "good-bye" held the promise of a lusty "hello." It got to the point that you dressed for everyone of these events with him in mind. Every body-enhancing dress, every spritz of perfume, every pair of stiletto, come-fuck-me shoes, was chosen with the hope that he would be there, that he would notice, find you across the room and look into your eyes, smile that wicked smile, and be your hot-ass fantasy for the rest of the week.

You knew this fine financier was unmarried, but he always showed up at these events with the same woman, so you assumed that he was happily attached. You also assumed that your sexy attraction to him was one sided, so you did nothing, said nothing, implied nothing. As far as you were concerned he was your secret fantasy and that was all it would ever amount to.

That is until Nelson Mandela came to town. God bless that man. His masterful legacy of orchestrating his nation's transition from apartheid to democracy not only freed a people, but was the catalyst in you gaining your sexual freedom as well. True, no match in the big scheme of things, but in the small corner of your little world it felt like a global event. Had Mr.

Mandela not come to Radio City Music Hall to celebrate the first International Mandela Day with his supportive and proud American brethren, your lust, your love, your life would have been forever imprisoned.

It was there, in the ballroom of the lobby of the concert hall, that he, Mr. Killer Smile, appeared by your side and spoke the words that set destiny in motion and led you to this spot today in midtown Manhattan: "I can fuck for hours without coming," he said matter-of-factly. "And right now I want my dick deep inside your pussy."

Now, another place, another time, another mouth, you would have been highly offended. But not this night. Not with this man. You were two people with like minds. You smiled and gently bit your lower lip, something you tend to do when you are very turned on, but unfortunately, no other words were exchanged as his escort appeared and whisked him off to take their seats. You were left there alone, desire dripping down your legs.

In the six days that have passed, you have replayed those words at least ten times a day in your head. You have driven yourself mad with wonder, with wilting willpower, and gone wild with lust. You want this man. And this is the day you will have him.

So here you are at 2:53 p.m., standing on the sidewalk in front of his office building. He has no idea that his three o'clock appointment is with you. You are about to walk into his office, wearing nothing but black heels and a sheer red bra and matching panties under your coat, and have your way with the man whom you have spent months fantasizing about. You are tired of taking things into your own hands. The phantom fuck is over. Today, it's about the real thing. Today, it will be *his* hands, not yours, *his* mouth, *his* tongue, *his* dick bringing you to orgasm.

You walk purposefully through the lobby and gratefully find yourself alone in the elevator. The doors close and the thought of ascending into his space sends a gush of longing through your body. Desire leads your hands inside your coat and you fondle your nipples in preparation. They immediately react, becoming hard and sending electric currents to your clit. It's a long ride to the seventy-fourth floor and your pussy is demanding attention, so you pull a two-inch bullet vibrator from your pocket and tuck it into your G-string, placing it directly on your engorged bud. You squeeze your legs and do a few quick kegels, causing your ass to clench and pelvis to push forward in search of his dick. Your nipples continue to react to your twisting and pulling, causing your sex muscles to twitch and jump even more.

"Yeah, time to put that dick deep into my pussy, mother-fucker," you inform him telepathically as you picture his throbbing stick knocking at your G-spot's door. The combination of contraction and vibration and nasty thoughts has you at orgasm's threshold, but you do not want to come yet. Not without him. Not again.

You disengage the bullet and pull it, awash in pussy juice, from your panties. By the time the lift deposits you on his floor you are wet and waaay beyond ready to fuck the shit out of this sexy-ass man. You announce your arrival to the receptionist, and stand as she calls his office, all the while wondering if she can smell the scent of an aroused kitty.

"He says go right in," she announces.

You slowly walk the length of the corridor, anticipation guiding each deliberate step. You feel good, invincible and sexy as hell as you lightly tap on his door. The temptation is over. Redemption is at hand.

"Come in," he says, too busy standing up and buttoning

his suit jacket to really notice who has just appeared across his threshold.

"Hi," you say softly, catching his gaze and locking focus. He's surprised. It is obvious by the momentary shock in his eyes. But pleased. The twitch in the corner of his mouth pulling his lips upright is proof.

"Have a seat. May I take your coat?"

Please do continue...

LEAD ME INTO TEMPTATION…

STREET LOVE

I couldn't leave without you," the words drifting through the darkness inform me.

I pull my jacket tight across my chest, protection not only from the cool night air, but the chill that her voice sends through me. I step farther onto the desolate sidewalk and turn toward the sound of her voice.

"I'm here, waiting for you," she continues, providing the verbal bread crumbs I need to follow and find her. "This way."

Like a beacon, a white rose appears, jutting from the side of the building. I continue to walk, hearing the clack of high heels blend with the beat of my heart as I progress. I make the turn at the edge of the edifice and gingerly reach for the bloom. Instead of a flower, my hand meets flesh as she grabs and pulls me to her. In the darkness, I cannot make out her face, but the smells, sounds and feel of her assure me this is Cameron. She gives me the rose before clasping both of her hands in mine and gently but forcefully pinning them to her side.

The urge to protest melts under the heat of her kiss. Cameron's mouth burns into mine without polite pretense, and unlike earlier when our lips met in quiet discovery, this kiss is fueled by an overwhelming passion demanding to be satisfied. With a hunger indicative of starvation, Cameron begins making a feast of my eyes, nose, cheeks and earlobes before once again devouring my mouth. Her tongue penetrates my lips, at first a relaxed tool of sensual seduction and then becoming stiff and hard, thrusting in and out in a sexy demonstration of things to come.

My breath becomes short and labored as she presses her body against mine. She can feel the hardness on my thigh and it excites her. Words have no place in this conversation, and feeling flushed and heated by the blood rushing through my body and pooling between my legs, I express myself with a low whimper that caresses her ears and heightens her desire.

Cameron releases my hands in order to slide the cashmere jacket from my shoulders. It is dropped to the pavement without concern. Her lips graze my ear and counting aloud as each one falls open, I undo the six oversized, white buttons running down her blouse and into the top of her skirt. Once they're unfastened, I release the hem from her waistband and peel away the shirt, sending it fluttering to the ground to join her jacket.

"You are beautiful," I murmur in admiration as I take in her copious breasts covered in a sheer white bra edged in taupe lace. It is a look that is as innocent as it is crazy sexy.

Cameron reaches down, takes the rose from my hand, and holds it to my nose. I close my eyes and take a deep breath, inhaling its subtle and seductive aroma. It smells like her—erotically innocent. I respond with an open mouth exhale, prompting Cameron to drag the bloom slowly down my mouth, causing the delicately curled petals to catch and tickle my swollen lips.

I take possession of this love bloom and continue the seductive journey down her neck and across her shoulders, sweeping the velvety softness of the petals across the full tops of her breasts, bringing forth another delicious moan. Their silkiness teases every nerve ending, causing her entire body to tingle in reaction. Enjoying her pleasure, I brush the rose against the sheer whisper of material separating her skin from my touch. Her nipples stiffen in response, a reaction I no longer have the fortitude to ignore.

My mouth impatiently retraces the rose-petal trail across her bosom. I latch on, bathing her nipples in warm saliva, my actions simultaneously drenching both her bra and panties. With one hand, I reach up and into her brassiere, releasing her breasts as I continue my erotic tongue and hand massage. I nibble and knead with practiced expertise until Cameron announces her escalating excitement with a primitive groan. Encouraged, I linger, pushing her breasts together and rolling both nipples gently between my teeth until Cam arches her back and presses herself against me, trying to find relief for the intensifying ache in her pelvis.

Not yet ready to surrender to my craving, I pull back and petal by petal, begin to dismantle the blossom. A shower of white floral confetti rains down on us, sticking to her body and coating the ground below. I pluck a petal from her hair and use it to tease her naked nipples to attention. Cameron feels the cool gossamer touch and immediately the bud between her legs begins to contract. She exhales loudly, a reaction to the exquisite pain of unsatisfied arousal.

Unable to contain herself, Cameron pushes me against the brick wall. Logic-blocking waves of desire keep me from protesting. All inhibition is lost. Neither she nor I care who sees us—the girl, the photographers, the public—nothing matters but having each other. Right here. And right now.

I pull up her skirt, only to find the cure for my lust obstructed by the same delicate material that had covered her breasts. I release her panties from her hips, causing them to slide down her legs, stopping at her ankles. Cam spreads her legs wider as I slide my hand between them, coaxing her lower lips apart with my fingers. Lifting the other hand to her head, I lift a rose petal from her hair and swipe her milky desire before using it to massage her bud, rubbing both and releasing into the air the sweet-scented essence of rose mixed with her sex.

"Fuck me. Please. Now," she demands.

I smile. She is impatient to have me. I like my women hot and hungry. They complement my patience and endurance. The combination guarantees lots of long fucking sessions.

I push two fingers high inside her, twisting like a corkscrew, trying to hit every nerve I can find. I pull out and twist my hand before reentering her and pushing wrist-deep, searching for her G-spot. My hand is too small, so once again I exit, wiping pussy juice across her naked tits and then putting what's left on my thirsty tongue. I take from my trouser pocket the hard shaft she desires, shoving it into her pussy and thrusting it back and forth with building speed. My lips reclaim her hard nipples and I suck hard, determined to pull from her an orgasm that will have her seeing stars beyond the Milky Way.

"Come for me, bitch." I demand. "Come for me hard and then you are going to drop to your knees and eat my pussy like it is the last thing on earth you will ever taste."

Hearing me, Cameron explodes into orgasm, her screams echoing through the streets. I pull the dildo from her and suck her sweet juices as I fall back against the bricks, ready for release, and wait for her to recover. Cameron quickly unbuttons my shirt to find me braless with nipples erect. She rubs her tits against mine as she unzips my pants and pushes them down to my ankles. Her tongue leaves a trail of saliva from my breasts to my waiting mound. Cam latches on to the engorged button, perfectly applying both fierce and fragile suction. Her tongue laps around and around my nib as her fingers vibrate up and down inside my hole. I hear the sounds of the city around me, but they cannot distract me from my mission.

"I leave you alone for ten minutes and you're out fucking some other bitch. Do I need to put a leash on you?" Sasha asks, suddenly appearing to grab Cam's arm and pull her away from me. I am left feeling unnerved and totally unsatisfied.

"Cameron!" I call out as she quickly gathers her belongings and scurries away, my nectar still dripping down her chin. She stops and turns, her face a billboard of uncertainty.

Please do continue...